The Lady of the Lake

by

Sir Walter Scott, Bart.

The Lady of the Lake

Walter Scott

DODO PRESS

THE LADY OF THE LAKE.

CANTO FIRST.

The Chase.

Harp of the North! that mouldering long hast hung
On the witch-elm that shades Saint Fillan's spring
And down the fitful breeze thy numbers flung,
Till envious ivy did around thee cling,
Muffling with verdant ringlet every string,--
O Minstrel Harp, still must thine accents sleep?
Mid rustling leaves and fountains murmuring,
Still must thy sweeter sounds their silence keep,
Nor bid a warrior smile, nor teach a maid to weep?

Not thus, in ancient days of Caledon,
Was thy voice mute amid the festal crowd,
When lay of hopeless love, or glory won,
Aroused the fearful or subdued the proud.
At each according pause was heard aloud
Thine ardent symphony sublime and high!
Fair dames and crested chiefs attention bowed;
For still the burden of thy minstrelsy
Was Knighthood's dauntless deed, and Beauty's matchless eye.

O, wake once more! how rude soe'er the hand
That ventures o'er thy magic maze to stray;
O, wake once more! though scarce my skill command
Some feeble echoing of thine earlier lay:
Though harsh and faint, and soon to die away,
And all unworthy of thy nobler strain,
Yet if one heart throb higher at its sway,
The wizard note has not been touched in vain.
Then silent be no more! Enchantress, wake again!

The Lady of the Lake

I.

The stag at eve had drunk his fill,
Where danced the moon on Monan's rill,
And deep his midnight lair had made
In lone Glenartney's hazel shade;
But when the sun his beacon red
Had kindled on Benvoirlich's head,
The deep-mouthed bloodhound's heavy bay
Resounded up the rocky way,
And faint, from farther distance borne,
Were heard the clanging hoof and horn.

II.

As Chief, who hears his warder call,
'To arms! the foemen storm the wall,'
The antlered monarch of the waste
Sprung from his heathery couch in haste.
But ere his fleet career he took,
The dew-drops from his flanks he shook;
Like crested leader proud and high
Tossed his beamed frontlet to the sky;
A moment gazed adown the dale,
A moment snuffed the tainted gale,
A moment listened to the cry,
That thickened as the chase drew nigh;
Then, as the headmost foes appeared,
With one brave bound the copse he cleared,
And, stretching forward free and far,
Sought the wild heaths of Uam-Var.

III.

Yelled on the view the opening pack;
Rock, glen, and cavern paid them back;
To many a mingled sound at once
The awakened mountain gave response.
A hundred dogs bayed deep and strong,
Clattered a hundred steeds along,
Their peal the merry horns rung out,

A hundred voices joined the shout;
With hark and whoop and wild halloo,
No rest Benvoirlich's echoes knew.
Far from the tumult fled the roe,
Close in her covert cowered the doe,
The falcon, from her cairn on high,
Cast on the rout a wondering eye,
Till far beyond her piercing ken
The hurricane had swept the glen.
Faint, and more faint, its failing din
Returned from cavern, cliff, and linn,
And silence settled, wide and still,
On the lone wood and mighty hill.

IV.

Less loud the sounds of sylvan war
Disturbed the heights of Uam-Var,
And roused the cavern where, 't is told,
A giant made his den of old;
For ere that steep ascent was won,
High in his pathway hung the sun,
And many a gallant, stayed perforce,
Was fain to breathe his faltering horse,
And of the trackers of the deer
Scarce half the lessening pack was near;
So shrewdly on the mountain-side
Had the bold burst their mettle tried.

V.

The noble stag was pausing now
Upon the mountain's southern brow,
Where broad extended, far beneath,
The varied realms of fair Menteith.
With anxious eye he wandered o'er
Mountain and meadow, moss and moor,
And pondered refuge from his toil,
By far Lochard or Aberfoyle.
But nearer was the copsewood gray
That waved and wept on Loch Achray,

And mingled with the pine-trees blue
On the bold cliffs of Benvenue.
Fresh vigor with the hope returned,
With flying foot the heath he spurned,
Held westward with unwearied race,
And left behind the panting chase.

VI.

'T were long to tell what steeds gave o'er,
As swept the hunt through Cambusmore;
What reins were tightened in despair,
When rose Benledi's ridge in air;
Who flagged upon Bochastle's heath,
Who shunned to stem the flooded Teith,--
For twice that day, from shore to shore,
The gallant stag swam stoutly o'er.
Few were the stragglers, following far,
That reached the lake of Vennachar;
And when the Brigg of Turk was won,
The headmost horseman rode alone.

VII.

Alone, but with unbated zeal,
That horseman plied the scourge and steel;
For jaded now, and spent with toil,
Embossed with foam, and dark with soil,
While every gasp with sobs he drew,
The laboring stag strained full in view.
Two dogs of black Saint Hubert's breed,
Unmatched for courage, breath, and speed,
Fast on his flying traces came,
And all but won that desperate game;
For, scarce a spear's length from his haunch,
Vindictive toiled the bloodhounds stanch;
Nor nearer might the dogs attain,
Nor farther might the quarry strain
Thus up the margin of the lake,
Between the precipice and brake,
O'er stock and rock their race they take.

VIII.

The Hunter marked that mountain high,
The lone lake's western boundary,
And deemed the stag must turn to bay,
Where that huge rampart barred the way;
Already glorying in the prize,
Measured his antlers with his eyes;
For the death-wound and death-halloo
Mustered his breath, his whinyard drew:--
But thundering as he came prepared,
With ready arm and weapon bared,
The wily quarry shunned the shock,
And turned him from the opposing rock;
Then, dashing down a darksome glen,
Soon lost to hound and Hunter's ken,
In the deep Trosachs' wildest nook
His solitary refuge took.
There, while close couched the thicket shed
Cold dews and wild flowers on his head,
He heard the baffled dogs in vain
Rave through the hollow pass amain,
Chiding the rocks that yelled again.

IX.

Close on the hounds the Hunter came,
To cheer them on the vanished game;
But, stumbling in the rugged dell,
The gallant horse exhausted fell.
The impatient rider strove in vain
To rouse him with the spur and rein,
For the good steed, his labors o'er,
Stretched his stiff limbs, to rise no more;
Then, touched with pity and remorse,
He sorrowed o'er the expiring horse.
'I little thought, when first thy rein
I slacked upon the banks of Seine,
That Highland eagle e'er should feed
On thy fleet limbs, my matchless steed!

Woe worth the chase, woe worth the day,
That costs thy life, my gallant gray!'

X.

Then through the dell his horn resounds,
From vain pursuit to call the hounds.
Back limped, with slow and crippled pace,
The sulky leaders of the chase;
Close to their master's side they pressed,
With drooping tail and humbled crest;
But still the dingle's hollow throat
Prolonged the swelling bugle-note.
The owlets started from their dream,
The eagles answered with their scream,
Round and around the sounds were cast,
Till echo seemed an answering blast;
And on the Hunter tried his way,
To join some comrades of the day,
Yet often paused, so strange the road,
So wondrous were the scenes it showed.

XI.

The western waves of ebbing day
Rolled o'er the glen their level way;
Each purple peak, each flinty spire,
Was bathed in floods of living fire.
But not a setting beam could glow
Within the dark ravines below,
Where twined the path in shadow hid,
Round many a rocky pyramid,
Shooting abruptly from the dell
Its thunder-splintered pinnacle;
Round many an insulated mass,
The native bulwarks of the pass,
Huge as the tower which builders vain
Presumptuous piled on Shinar's plain.
The rocky summits, split and rent,
Formed turret, dome, or battlement.
Or seemed fantastically set

With cupola or minaret,
Wild crests as pagod ever decked,
Or mosque of Eastern architect.
Nor were these earth-born castles bare,
Nor lacked they many a banner fair;
For, from their shivered brows displayed,
Far o'er the unfathomable glade,
All twinkling with the dewdrop sheen,
The briar-rose fell in streamers green,
kind creeping shrubs of thousand dyes
Waved in the west-wind's summer sighs.

XII.

Boon nature scattered, free and wild,
Each plant or flower, the mountain's child.
Here eglantine embalmed the air,
Hawthorn and hazel mingled there;
The primrose pale and violet flower
Found in each cliff a narrow bower;
Foxglove and nightshade, side by side,
Emblems of punishment and pride,
Grouped their dark hues with every stain
The weather-beaten crags retain.
With boughs that quaked at every breath,
Gray birch and aspen wept beneath;
Aloft, the ash and warrior oak
Cast anchor in the rifted rock;
And, higher yet, the pine-tree hung
His shattered trunk, and frequent flung,
Where seemed the cliffs to meet on high,
His boughs athwart the narrowed sky.
Highest of all, where white peaks glanced,
Where glistening streamers waved and danced,
The wanderer's eye could barely view
The summer heaven's delicious blue;
So wondrous wild, the whole might seem
The scenery of a fairy dream.

XIII.

Onward, amid the copse 'gan peep
A narrow inlet, still and deep,
Affording scarce such breadth of brim
As served the wild duck's brood to swim.
Lost for a space, through thickets veering,
But broader when again appearing,
Tall rocks and tufted knolls their face
Could on the dark-blue mirror trace;
And farther as the Hunter strayed,
Still broader sweep its channels made.
The shaggy mounds no longer stood,
Emerging from entangled wood,
But, wave-encircled, seemed to float,
Like castle girdled with its moat;
Yet broader floods extending still
Divide them from their parent hill,
Till each, retiring, claims to be
An islet in an inland sea.

XIV.

And now, to issue from the glen,
No pathway meets the wanderer's ken,
Unless he climb with footing nice
A far-projecting precipice.
The broom's tough roots his ladder made,
The hazel saplings lent their aid;
And thus an airy point he won,
Where, gleaming with the setting sun,
One burnished sheet of living gold,
Loch Katrine lay beneath him rolled,
In all her length far winding lay,
With promontory, creek, and bay,
And islands that, empurpled bright,
Floated amid the livelier light,
And mountains that like giants stand
To sentinel enchanted land.
High on the south, huge Benvenue
Down to the lake in masses threw
Crags, knolls, and mounds, confusedly hurled,
The fragments of an earlier world;
A wildering forest feathered o'er

His ruined sides and summit hoar,
While on the north, through middle air,
Ben-an heaved high his forehead bare.

XV.

From the steep promontory gazed
The stranger, raptured and amazed,
And, 'What a scene were here,' he cried,
'For princely pomp or churchman's pride!
On this bold brow, a lordly tower;
In that soft vale, a lady's bower;
On yonder meadow far away,
The turrets of a cloister gray;
How blithely might the bugle-horn
Chide on the lake the lingering morn!
How sweet at eve the lover's lute
Chime when the groves were still and mute!
And when the midnight moon should lave
Her forehead in the silver wave,
How solemn on the ear would come
The holy matins' distant hum,
While the deep peal's commanding tone
Should wake, in yonder islet lone,
A sainted hermit from his cell,
To drop a bead with every knell!
And bugle, lute, and bell, and all,
Should each bewildered stranger call
To friendly feast and lighted hall.

XVI.

'Blithe were it then to wander here!
But now--beshrew yon nimble deer--
Like that same hermit's, thin and spare,
The copse must give my evening fare;
Some mossy bank my couch must be,
Some rustling oak my canopy.
Yet pass we that; the war and chase
Give little choice of resting-place;--
A summer night in greenwood spent

Were but to-morrow's merriment:
But hosts may in these wilds abound,
Such as are better missed than found;
To meet with Highland plunderers here
Were worse than loss of steed or deer.--
I am alone;--my bugle-strain
May call some straggler of the train;
Or, fall the worst that may betide,
Ere now this falchion has been tried.'

XVII.

But scarce again his horn he wound,
When lo! forth starting at the sound,
From underneath an aged oak
That slanted from the islet rock,
A damsel guider of its way,
A little skiff shot to the bay,
That round the promontory steep
Led its deep line in graceful sweep,
Eddying, in almost viewless wave,
The weeping willow twig to rave,
And kiss, with whispering sound and slow,
The beach of pebbles bright as snow.
The boat had touched this silver strand
Just as the Hunter left his stand,
And stood concealed amid the brake,
To view this Lady of the Lake.
The maiden paused, as if again
She thought to catch the distant strain.
With head upraised, and look intent,
And eye and ear attentive bent,
And locks flung back, and lips apart,
Like monument of Grecian art,
In listening mood, she seemed to stand,
The guardian Naiad of the strand.

XVIII.

And ne'er did Grecian chisel trace
A Nymph, a Naiad, or a Grace,

Of finer form or lovelier face!
What though the sun, with ardent frown,
Had slightly tinged her cheek with brown,--
The sportive toil, which, short and light
Had dyed her glowing hue so bright,
Served too in hastier swell to show
Short glimpses of a breast of snow:
What though no rule of courtly grace
To measured mood had trained her pace,--
A foot more light, a step more true,
Ne'er from the heath-flower dashed the dew;
E'en the slight harebell raised its head,
Elastic from her airy tread:
What though upon her speech there hung
The accents of the mountain tongue,---
Those silver sounds, so soft, so dear,
The listener held his breath to hear!

XIX.

A chieftain's daughter seemed the maid;
Her satin snood, her silken plaid,
Her golden brooch, such birth betrayed.
And seldom was a snood amid
Such wild luxuriant ringlets hid,
Whose glossy black to shame might bring
The plumage of the raven's wing;
And seldom o'er a breast so fair
Mantled a plaid with modest care,
And never brooch the folds combined
Above a heart more good and kind.
Her kindness and her worth to spy,
You need but gaze on Ellen's eye;
Not Katrine in her mirror blue
Gives back the shaggy banks more true,
Than every free-born glance confessed
The guileless movements of her breast;
Whether joy danced in her dark eye,
Or woe or pity claimed a sigh,
Or filial love was glowing there,
Or meek devotion poured a prayer,
Or tale of injury called forth

The indignant spirit of the North.
One only passion unrevealed
With maiden pride the maid concealed,
Yet not less purely felt the flame;--
O, need I tell that passion's name?

XX.

Impatient of the silent horn,
Now on the gale her voice was borne:--
'Father!' she cried; the rocks around
Loved to prolong the gentle sound.
Awhile she paused, no answer came;--
'Malcolm, was thine the blast?' the name
Less resolutely uttered fell,
The echoes could not catch the swell.
'A stranger I,' the Huntsman said,
Advancing from the hazel shade.
The maid, alarmed, with hasty oar
Pushed her light shallop from the shore,
And when a space was gained between,
Closer she drew her bosom's screen;--
So forth the startled swan would swing,
So turn to prune his ruffled wing.
Then safe, though fluttered and amazed,
She paused, and on the stranger gazed.
Not his the form, nor his the eye,
That youthful maidens wont to fly.

XXI.

On his bold visage middle age
Had slightly pressed its signet sage,
Yet had not quenched the open truth
And fiery vehemence of youth;
Forward and frolic glee was there,
The will to do, the soul to dare,
The sparkling glance, soon blown to fire,
Of hasty love or headlong ire.
His limbs were cast in manly could
For hardy sports or contest bold;

And though in peaceful garb arrayed,
And weaponless except his blade,
His stately mien as well implied
A high-born heart, a martial pride,
As if a baron's crest he wore,
And sheathed in armor bode the shore.
Slighting the petty need he showed,
He told of his benighted road;
His ready speech flowed fair and free,
In phrase of gentlest courtesy,
Yet seemed that tone and gesture bland
Less used to sue than to command.

XXII.

Awhile the maid the stranger eyed,
And, reassured, at length replied,
That Highland halls were open still
To wildered wanderers of the hill.
'Nor think you unexpected come
To yon lone isle, our desert home;
Before the heath had lost the dew,
This morn, a couch was pulled for you;
On yonder mountain's purple head
Have ptarmigan and heath-cock bled,
And our broad nets have swept the mere,
To furnish forth your evening cheer.'--
'Now, by the rood, my lovely maid,
Your courtesy has erred,' he said;
'No right have I to claim, misplaced,
The welcome of expected guest.
A wanderer, here by fortune toss,
My way, my friends, my courser lost,
I ne'er before, believe me, fair,
Have ever drawn your mountain air,
Till on this lake's romantic strand
I found a fey in fairy land!'--

XXIII.

'I well believe,' the maid replied,

As her light skiff approached the side,--
'I well believe, that ne'er before
Your foot has trod Loch Katrine's shore
But yet, as far as yesternight,
Old Allan-bane foretold your plight,--
A gray -haired sire, whose eye intent
Was on the visioned future bent.
He saw your steed, a dappled gray,
Lie dead beneath the birchen way;
Painted exact your form and mien,
Your hunting-suit of Lincoln green,
That tasselled horn so gayly gilt,
That falchion's crooked blade and hilt,
That cap with heron plumage trim,
And yon two hounds so dark and grim.
He bade that all should ready be
To grace a guest of fair degree;
But light I held his prophecy,
And deemed it was my father's horn
Whose echoes o'er the lake were borne.'

XXIV.

The stranger smiled: -- 'Since to your home
A destined errant-knight I come,
Announced by prophet sooth and old,
Doomed, doubtless, for achievement bold,
I 'll lightly front each high emprise
For one kind glance of those bright eyes.
Permit me first the task to guide
Your fairy frigate o'er the tide.'
The maid, with smile suppressed and sly,
The toil unwonted saw him try;
For seldom, sure, if e'er before,
His noble hand had grasped an oar:
Yet with main strength his strokes he drew,
And o'er the lake the shallop flew;
With heads erect and whimpering cry,
The hounds behind their passage ply.
Nor frequent does the bright oar break
The darkening mirror of the lake,
Until the rocky isle they reach,

And moor their shallop on the beach.

XXV.

The stranger viewed the shore around;
'T was all so close with copsewood bound,
Nor track nor pathway might declare
That human foot frequented there,
Until the mountain maiden showed
A clambering unsuspected road,
That winded through the tangled screen,
And opened on a narrow green,
Where weeping birch and willow round
With their long fibres swept the ground.
Here, for retreat in dangerous hour,
Some chief had framed a rustic bower.

XXVI.

It was a lodge of ample size,
But strange of structure and device;
Of such materials as around
The workman's hand had readiest found.
Lopped of their boughs, their hoar trunks bared,
And by the hatchet rudely squared,
To give the walls their destined height,
The sturdy oak and ash unite;
While moss and clay and leaves combined
To fence each crevice from the wind.
The lighter pine-trees overhead
Their slender length for rafters spread,
And withered heath and rushes dry
Supplied a russet canopy.
Due westward, fronting to the green,
A rural portico was seen,
Aloft on native pillars borne,
Of mountain fir with bark unshorn
Where Ellen's hand had taught to twine
The ivy and Idaean vine,
The clematis, the favored flower
Which boasts the name of virgin-bower,

And every hardy plant could bear
Loch Katrine's keen and searching air.
An instant in this porch she stayed,
And gayly to the stranger said:
'On heaven and on thy lady call,
And enter the enchanted hall!'

XXVII.

'My hope, my heaven, my trust must be,
My gentle guide, in following thee!'--
He crossed the threshold,--and a clang
Of angry steel that instant rang.
To his bold brow his spirit rushed,
But soon for vain alarm he blushed
When on the floor he saw displayed,
Cause of the din, a naked blade
Dropped from the sheath, that careless flung
Upon a stag's huge antlers swung;
For all around, the walls to grace,
Hung trophies of the fight or chase:
A target there, a bugle here,
A battle-axe, a hunting-spear,
And broadswords, bows, and arrows store,
With the tusked trophies of the boar.
Here grins the wolf as when he died,
And there the wild-cat's brindled hide
The frontlet of the elk adorns,
Or mantles o'er the bison's horns;
Pennons and flags defaced and stained,
That blackening streaks of blood retained,
And deer-skins, dappled, dun, and white,
With otter's fur and seal's unite,
In rude and uncouth tapestry all,
To garnish forth the sylvan hall.

XXVIII.

The wondering stranger round him gazed,
And next the fallen weapon raised:--
Few were the arms whose sinewy strength

Sufficed to stretch it forth at length.
And as the brand he poised and swayed,
'I never knew but one,' he said,
'Whose stalwart arm might brook to wield
A blade like this in battle-field.'
She sighed, then smiled and took the word:
'You see the guardian champion's sword;
As light it trembles in his hand
As in my grasp a hazel wand:
My sire's tall form might grace the part
Of Ferragus or Ascabart,
But in the absent giant's hold
Are women now, and menials old.'

XXIX.

The mistress of the mansion came,
Mature of age, a graceful dame,
Whose easy step and stately port
Had well become a princely court,
To whom, though more than kindred knew,
Young Ellen gave a mother's due.
Meet welcome to her guest she made,
And every courteous rite was paid
That hospitality could claim,
Though all unasked his birth and name.
Such then the reverence to a guest,
That fellest foe might join the feast,
And from his deadliest foeman's door
Unquestioned turn the banquet o'er
At length his rank the stranger names,
'The Knight of Snowdoun, James Fitz-James;
Lord of a barren heritage,
Which his brave sires, from age to age,
By their good swords had held with toil;
His sire had fallen in such turmoil,
And he, God wot, was forced to stand
Oft for his right with blade in hand.
This morning with Lord Moray's train
He chased a stalwart stag in vain,
Outstripped his comrades, missed the deer,
Lost his good steed, and wandered here.'

XXX.

Fain would the Knight in turn require
The name and state of Ellen's sire.
Well showed the elder lady's mien
That courts and cities she had seen;
Ellen, though more her looks displayed
The simple grace of sylvan maid,
In speech and gesture, form and face,
Showed she was come of gentle race.
'T were strange in ruder rank to find
Such looks, such manners, and such mind.
Each hint the Knight of Snowdoun gave,
Dame Margaret heard with silence grave;
Or Ellen, innocently gay,
Turned all inquiry light away:--
'Weird women we! by dale and down
We dwell, afar from tower and town.
We stem the flood, we ride the blast,
On wandering knights our spells we cast;
While viewless minstrels touch the string,
'Tis thus our charmed rhymes we sing.'
She sung, and still a harp unseen
Filled up the symphony between.

XXXI.

Song.

Soldier, rest! thy warfare o'er,
Sleep the sleep that knows not breaking;
Dream of battled fields no more,
Days of danger, nights of waking.
In our isle's enchanted hall,
Hands unseen thy couch are strewing,
Fairy strains of music fall,
Every sense in slumber dewing.
Soldier, rest! thy warfare o'er,
Dream of fighting fields no more;
Sleep the sleep that knows not breaking,

Morn of toil, nor night of waking.

'No rude sound shall reach thine ear,
Armor's clang or war-steed champing
Trump nor pibroch summon here
Mustering clan or squadron tramping.
Yet the lark's shrill fife may come
At the daybreak from the fallow,
And the bittern sound his drum
Booming from the sedgy shallow.
Ruder sounds shall none be near,
Guards nor warders challenge here,
Here's no war-steed's neigh and champing,
Shouting clans or squadrons stamping.'

XXXII.

She paused,--then, blushing, led the lay,
To grace the stranger of the day.
Her mellow notes awhile prolong
The cadence of the flowing song,
Till to her lips in measured frame
The minstrel verse spontaneous came.

Song Continued.

'Huntsman, rest! thy chase is done;
While our slumbrous spells assail ye,
Dream not, with the rising sun,
Bugles here shall sound reveille.
Sleep! the deer is in his den;
Sleep! thy hounds are by thee lying;
Sleep! nor dream in yonder glen
How thy gallant steed lay dying.
Huntsman, rest! thy chase is done;
Think not of the rising sun,
For at dawning to assail ye
Here no bugles sound reveille.'

XXXIII.

The hall was cleared,--- the stranger's bed,
Was there of mountain heather spread,
Where oft a hundred guests had lain,
And dreamed their forest sports again.
But vainly did the heath-flower shed
Its moorland fragrance round his head;
Not Ellen's spell had lulled to rest
The fever of his troubled breast.
In broken dreams the image rose
Of varied perils, pains, and woes:
His steed now flounders in the brake,
Now sinks his barge upon the lake;
Now leader of a broken host,
His standard falls, his honor's lost.
Then,--from my couch may heavenly might
Chase that worst phantom of the night!--
Again returned the scenes of youth,
Of confident, undoubting truth;
Again his soul he interchanged
With friends whose hearts were long estranged.
They come, in dim procession led,
The cold, the faithless, and the dead;
As warm each hand, each brow as gay,
As if they parted yesterday.
And doubt distracts him at the view,--
O were his senses false or true?
Dreamed he of death or broken vow,
Or is it all a vision now?

XXXIV.

At length, with Ellen in a grove
He seemed to walk and speak of love;
She listened with a blush and sigh,
His suit was warm, his hopes were high.
He sought her yielded hand to clasp,
And a cold gauntlet met his grasp:
The phantom's sex was changed and gone,
Upon its head a helmet shone;
Slowly enlarged to giant size,
With darkened cheek and threatening eyes,
The grisly visage, stern and hoar,

To Ellen still a likeness bore.--
He woke, and, panting with affright,
Recalled the vision of the night.
The hearth's decaying brands were red
And deep and dusky lustre shed,
Half showing, half concealing, all
The uncouth trophies of the hall.
Mid those the stranger fixed his eye
Where that huge falchion hung on high,
And thoughts on thoughts, a countless throng,
Rushed, chasing countless thoughts along,
Until, the giddy whirl to cure,
He rose and sought the moonshine pure.

XXXV.

The wild rose, eglantine, and broom
Wasted around their rich perfume;
The birch-trees wept in fragrant balm;
The aspens slept beneath the calm;
The silver light, with quivering glance,
Played on the water's still expanse,--
Wild were the heart whose passion's sway
Could rage beneath the sober ray!
He felt its calm, that warrior guest,
While thus he communed with his breast:--
'Why is it, at each turn I trace
Some memory of that exiled race?
Can I not mountain maiden spy,
But she must bear the Douglas eye?
Can I not view a Highland brand,
But it must match the Douglas hand?
Can I not frame a fevered dream,
But still the Douglas is the theme?
I'll dream no more,-- by manly mind
Not even in sleep is will resigned.
My midnight orisons said o'er,
I'll turn to rest, and dream no more.'
His midnight orisons he told,
A prayer with every bead of gold,
Consigned to heaven his cares and woes,
And sunk in undisturbed repose,

CANTO SECOND.

The Island.

I.

At morn the black-cock trims his jetty wing,
'T is morning prompts the linnet's blithest lay,
All Nature's children feel the matin spring
Of life reviving, with reviving day;
And while yon little bark glides down the bay,
Wafting the stranger on his way again,
Morn's genial influence roused a minstrel gray,
And sweetly o'er the lake was heard thy strain,
Mixed with the sounding harp, O white-haired Allan-bane!

II.

Song.

'Not faster yonder rowers' might
Flings from their oars the spray,
Not faster yonder rippling bright,
That tracks the shallop's course in light,
Melts in the lake away,
Than men from memory erase
The benefits of former days;
Then, stranger, go! good speed the while,
Nor think again of the lonely isle.

'High place to thee in royal court,
High place in battled line,
Good hawk and hound for sylvan sport!
Where beauty sees the brave resort,
The honored meed be thine!
True be thy sword, thy friend sincere,
Thy lady constant, kind, and dear,
And lost in love's and friendship's smile
Be memory of the lonely isle!

III.

Song Continued.

'But if beneath yon southern sky
A plaided stranger roam,
Whose drooping crest and stifled sigh,
And sunken cheek and heavy eye,
Pine for his Highland home;
Then, warrior, then be thine to show
The care that soothes a wanderer's woe;
Remember then thy hap erewhile,
A stranger in the lonely isle.

'Or if on life's uncertain main
Mishap shall mar thy sail;
If faithful, wise, and brave in vain,
Woe, want, and exile thou sustain
Beneath the fickle gale;
Waste not a sigh on fortune changed,
On thankless courts, or friends estranged,
But come where kindred worth shall smile,
To greet thee in the lonely isle.'

IV.

As died the sounds upon the tide,
The shallop reached the mainland side,
And ere his onward way he took,
The stranger cast a lingering look,
Where easily his eye might reach
The Harper on the islet beach,
Reclined against a blighted tree,
As wasted, gray, and worn as he.
To minstrel meditation given,
His reverend brow was raised to heaven,
As from the rising sun to claim
A sparkle of inspiring flame.
His hand, reclined upon the wire,
Seemed watching the awakening fire;
So still he sat as those who wait
Till judgment speak the doom of fate;

So still, as if no breeze might dare
To lift one lock of hoary hair;
So still, as life itself were fled
In the last sound his harp had sped.

V.

Upon a rock with lichens wild,
Beside him Ellen sat and smiled.--
Smiled she to see the stately drake
Lead forth his fleet upon the lake,
While her vexed spaniel from the beach
Bayed at the prize beyond his reach?
Yet tell me, then, the maid who knows,
Why deepened on her cheek the rose?--
Forgive, forgive, Fidelity!
Perchance the maiden smiled to see
Yon parting lingerer wave adieu,
And stop and turn to wave anew;
And, lovely ladies, ere your ire
Condemn the heroine of my lyre,
Show me the fair would scorn to spy
And prize such conquest of her eve!

VI.

While yet he loitered on the spot,
It seemed as Ellen marked him not;
But when he turned him to the glade,
One courteous parting sign she made;
And after, oft the knight would say,
That not when prize of festal day
Was dealt him by the brightest fair
Who e'er wore jewel in her hair,
So highly did his bosom swell
As at that simple mute farewell.
Now with a trusty mountain-guide,
And his dark stag-hounds by his side,
He parts,--the maid, unconscious still,
Watched him wind slowly round the hill;
But when his stately form was hid,

The guardian in her bosom chid,--
'Thy Malcolm! vain and selfish maid!'
'T was thus upbraiding conscience said,--
'Not so had Malcolm idly hung
On the smooth phrase of Southern tongue;
Not so had Malcolm strained his eye
Another step than thine to spy.'--
'Wake, Allan-bane,' aloud she cried
To the old minstrel by her side,--
'Arouse thee from thy moody dream!
I 'll give thy harp heroic theme,
And warm thee with a noble name;
Pour forth the glory of the Graeme!'
Scarce from her lip the word had rushed,
When deep the conscious maiden blushed;
For of his clan, in hall and bower,
Young Malcolm Graeme was held the flower.

VII.

The minstrel waked his harp,--three times
Arose the well-known martial chimes,
And thrice their high heroic pride
In melancholy murmurs died.
'Vainly thou bidst, O noble maid,'
Clasping his withered hands, he said,
'Vainly thou bidst me wake the strain,
Though all unwont to bid in vain.
Alas! than mine a mightier hand
Has tuned my harp, my strings has spanned!
I touch the chords of joy, but low
And mournful answer notes of woe;
And the proud march which victors tread
Sinks in the wailing for the dead.
O, well for me, if mine alone
That dirge's deep prophetic tone!
If, as my tuneful fathers said,
This harp, which erst Saint Modan swayed,
Can thus its master's fate foretell,
Then welcome be the minstrel's knell.'

VIII.

'But ah! dear lady, thus it sighed,
The eve thy sainted mother died;
And such the sounds which, while I strove
To wake a lay of war or love,
Came marring all the festal mirth,
Appalling me who gave them birth,
And, disobedient to my call,
Wailed loud through Bothwell's bannered hall.
Ere Douglases, to ruin driven,
Were exiled from their native heaven.--
O! if yet worse mishap and woe
My master's house must undergo,
Or aught but weal to Ellen fair
Brood in these accents of despair,
No future bard, sad Harp! shall fling
Triumph or rapture from thy string;
One short, one final strain shall flow,
Fraught with unutterable woe,
Then shivered shall thy fragments lie,
Thy master cast him down and die!'

IX.

Soothing she answered him: 'Assuage,
Mine honored friend, the fears of age;
All melodies to thee are known
That harp has rung or pipe has blown,
In Lowland vale or Highland glen,
From Tweed to Spey--what marvel, then,
At times unbidden notes should rise,
Confusedly bound in memory's ties,
Entangling, as they rush along,
The war-march with the funeral song?--
Small ground is now for boding fear;
Obscure, but safe, we rest us here.
My sire, in native virtue great,
Resigning lordship, lands, and state,
Not then to fortune more resigned
Than yonder oak might give the wind;
The graceful foliage storms may reeve,

'Fine noble stem they cannot grieve.
For me'--she stooped, and, looking round,
Plucked a blue harebell from the ground,--
'For me, whose memory scarce conveys
An image of more splendid days,
This little flower that loves the lea
May well my simple emblem be;
It drinks heaven's dew as blithe as rose
That in the King's own garden grows;
And when I place it in my hair,
Allan, a bard is bound to swear
He ne'er saw coronet so fair.'
Then playfully the chaplet wild
She wreathed in her dark locks, and smiled.

X.

Her smile, her speech, with winning sway
Wiled the old Harper's mood away.
With such a look as hermits throw,
When angels stoop to soothe their woe
He gazed, till fond regret and pride
Thrilled to a tear, then thus replied:
'Loveliest and best! thou little know'st
The rank, the honors, thou hast lost!
O. might I live to see thee grace,
In Scotland's court, thy birthright place,
To see my favorite's step advance
The lightest in the courtly dance,
The cause of every gallant's sigh,
And leading star of every eye,
And theme of every minstrel's art,
The Lady of the Bleeding Heart!'

XI.

'Fair dreams are these,' the maiden cried,--
Light was her accent, yet she sighed,--
'Yet is this mossy rock to me
Worth splendid chair and canopy;
Nor would my footstep spring more gay

In courtly dance than blithe strathspey,
Nor half so pleased mine ear incline
To royal minstrel's lay as thine.
And then for suitors proud and high,
To bend before my conquering eye,--
Thou, flattering bard! thyself wilt say,
That grim Sir Roderick owns its sway.
The Saxon scourge, Clan- Alpine's pride,
The terror of Loch Lomond's side,
Would, at my suit, thou know'st, delay
A Lennox foray--for a day.'--

XII..

The ancient bard her glee repressed:
'Ill hast thou chosen theme for jest!
For who, through all this western wild,
Named Black Sir Roderick e'er, and smiled?
In Holy-Rood a knight he slew;
I saw, when back the dirk he drew,
Courtiers give place before the stride
Of the undaunted homicide;
And since, though outlawed, hath his hand
Full sternly kept his mountain land.

Who else dared give--ah! woe the day,
That I such hated truth should say!--
The Douglas, like a stricken deer,
Disowned by every noble peer,
Even the rude refuge we have here?
Alas, this wild marauding
Chief Alone might hazard our relief,
And now thy maiden charms expand,
Looks for his guerdon in thy hand;
Full soon may dispensation sought,
To back his suit, from Rome be brought.
Then, though an exile on the hill,
Thy father, as the Douglas, still
Be held in reverence and fear;
And though to Roderick thou'rt so dear
That thou mightst guide with silken thread.
Slave of thy will, this chieftain dread,

Yet, O loved maid, thy mirth refrain!
Thy hand is on a lion's mane.'--

XIII.

Minstrel,' the maid replied, and high
Her father's soul glanced from her eye,
'My debts to Roderick's house I know:
All that a mother could bestow
To Lady Margaret's care I owe,
Since first an orphan in the wild
She sorrowed o'er her sister's child;
To her brave chieftain son, from ire
Of Scotland's king who shrouds my sire,
A deeper, holier debt is owed;
And, could I pay it with my blood, Allan!
Sir Roderick should command
My blood, my life,--but not my hand.
Rather will Ellen Douglas dwell
A votaress in Maronnan's cell;
Rather through realms beyond the sea,
Seeking the world's cold charity
Where ne'er was spoke a Scottish word,
And ne'er the name of Douglas heard
An outcast pilgrim will she rove,
Than wed the man she cannot love.

XIV.

'Thou shak'st, good friend, thy tresses gray,--
That pleading look, what can it say
But what I own?--I grant him brave,
But wild as Bracklinn's thundering wave;
And generous, ---save vindictive mood
Or jealous transport chafe his blood:
I grant him true to friendly band,
As his claymore is to his hand;
But O! that very blade of steel
More mercy for a foe would feel:
I grant him liberal, to fling
Among his clan the wealth they bring,

When back by lake and glen they wind,
And in the Lowland leave behind,
Where once some pleasant hamlet stood,
A mass of ashes slaked with blood.
The hand that for my father fought
I honor, as his daughter ought;
But can I clasp it reeking red
From peasants slaughtered in their shed?
No! wildly while his virtues gleam,
They make his passions darker seem,
And flash along his spirit high,
Like lightning o'er the midnight sky.
While yet a child,--and children know,
Instinctive taught, the friend and foe,--
I shuddered at his brow of gloom,
His shadowy plaid and sable plume;
A maiden grown, I ill could bear
His haughty mien and lordly air:
But, if thou join'st a suitor's claim,
In serious mood, to Roderick's name.
I thrill with anguish! or, if e'er
A Douglas knew the word, with fear.
To change such odious theme were best,--
What think'st thou of our stranger guest? '--

XV.

'What think I of him?--woe the while
That brought such wanderer to our isle!
Thy father's battle-brand, of yore
For Tine-man forged by fairy lore,
What time he leagued, no longer foes
His Border spears with Hotspur's bows,
Did, self-unscabbarded, foreshow
The footstep of a secret foe.
If courtly spy hath harbored here,
What may we for the Douglas fear?
What for this island, deemed of old
Clan-Alpine's last and surest hold?
If neither spy nor foe, I pray
What yet may jealous Roderick say?--
Nay, wave not thy disdainful head!

Bethink thee of the discord dread
That kindled when at Beltane game
Thou least the dance with Malcolm Graeme;
Still, though thy sire the peace renewed
Smoulders in Roderick's breast the feud:
Beware!--But hark! what sounds are these?
My dull ears catch no faltering breeze
No weeping birch nor aspens wake,
Nor breath is dimpling in the lake;
Still is the canna's hoary beard,
Yet, by my minstrel faith, I heard--
And hark again! some pipe of war
Sends the hold pibroch from afar.'

XVI.

Far up the lengthened lake were spied
Four darkening specks upon the tide,
That, slow enlarging on the view,
Four manned and massed barges grew,
And, bearing downwards from Glengyle,
Steered full upon the lonely isle;
The point of Brianchoil they passed,
And, to the windward as they cast,
Against the sun they gave to shine
The bold Sir Roderick's bannered Pine.
Nearer and nearer as they bear,
Spears, pikes, and axes flash in air.
Now might you see the tartars brave,
And plaids and plumage dance and wave:
Now see the bonnets sink and rise,
As his tough oar the rower plies;
See, flashing at each sturdy stroke,
The wave ascending into smoke;
See the proud pipers on the bow,
And mark the gaudy streamers flow
From their loud chanters down, and sweep
The furrowed bosom of the deep,
As, rushing through the lake amain,
They plied the ancient Highland strain.

XVII.

Ever, as on they bore, more loud
And louder rung the pibroch proud.
At first the sounds, by distance tame,
Mellowed along the waters came,
And, lingering long by cape and bay,
Wailed every harsher note away,
Then bursting bolder on the ear,
The clan's shrill Gathering they could hear,
Those thrilling sounds that call the might
Of old Clan-Alpine to the fight.
Thick beat the rapid notes, as when
The mustering hundreds shake the glen,
And hurrying at the signal dread,
'Fine battered earth returns their tread.
Then prelude light, of livelier tone,
Expressed their merry marching on,
Ere peal of closing battle rose,
With mingled outcry, shrieks, and blows;
And mimic din of stroke and ward,
As broadsword upon target jarred;
And groaning pause, ere yet again,
Condensed, the battle yelled amain:
The rapid charge, the rallying shout,
Retreat borne headlong into rout,
And bursts of triumph, to declare
Clan-Alpine's congest--all were there.
Nor ended thus the strain, but slow
Sunk in a moan prolonged and low,
And changed the conquering clarion swell
For wild lament o'er those that fell.

XVIII.

The war-pipes ceased, but lake and hill
Were busy with their echoes still;
And, when they slept, a vocal strain
Bade their hoarse chorus wake again,
While loud a hundred clansmen raise
Their voices in their Chieftain's praise.
Each boatman, bending to his oar,

With measured sweep the burden bore,
In such wild cadence as the breeze
Makes through December's leafless trees.
The chorus first could Allan know,
'Roderick Vich Alpine, ho! fro!'
And near, and nearer as they rowed,
Distinct the martial ditty flowed.

XIX.

Boat Song

Hail to the Chief who in triumph advances!
Honored and blessed be the ever-green Pine!
Long may the tree, in his banner that glances,
Flourish, the shelter and grace of our line!
Heaven send it happy dew,
Earth lend it sap anew,
Gayly to bourgeon and broadly to grow,
While every Highland glen
Sends our shout back again,
'Roderigh Vich Alpine dhu, ho! ieroe!'

Ours is no sapling, chance-sown by the fountain,

Blooming at Beltane, in winter to fade;
When the whirlwind has stripped every leaf on the mountain,
The more shall Clan-Alpine exult in her shade.
Moored in the rifted rock,
Proof to the tempest's shock,
Firmer he roots him the ruder it blow;
Menteith and Breadalbane, then,
Echo his praise again,
'Roderigh Vich Alpine dhu, ho! ieroe!'

XX.

Proudly our pibroch has thrilled in Glen Fruin,
And Bannochar's groans to our slogan replied;
Glen Luss and Ross-dhu, they are smoking in ruin,
And the best of Loch Lomond lie dead on her side.

Widow and Saxon maid
Long shall lament our raid,
Think of Clan-Alpine with fear and with woe;
Lennox and Leven-glen
Shake when they hear again,
'Roderigh Vich Alpine dhu, ho! ieroe!'

Row, vassals, row, for the pride of the Highlands!
Stretch to your oars for the ever-green Pine!
O that the rosebud that graces yon islands
Were wreathed in a garland around him to twine!
O that some seedling gem,
Worthy such noble stem,
Honored and blessed in their shadow might grow!
Loud should Clan-Alpine then
Ring from her deepmost glen,
Roderigh Vich Alpine dhu, ho! ieroe!'

XXI.

With all her joyful female band
Had Lady Margaret sought the strand.
Loose on the breeze their tresses flew,
And high their snowy arms they threw,
As echoing back with shrill acclaim,
And chorus wild, the Chieftain's name;
While, prompt to please, with mother's art
The darling passion of his heart,
The Dame called Ellen to the strand,
To greet her kinsman ere he land:
'Come, loiterer, come! a Douglas thou,
And shun to wreathe a victor's brow?'
Reluctantly and slow, the maid
The unwelcome summoning obeyed,
And when a distant bugle rung,
In the mid-path aside she sprung:--
'List, Allan-bane! From mainland cast
I hear my father's signal blast.
Be ours,' she cried, 'the skiff to guide,
And waft him from the mountain-side.'
Then, like a sunbeam, swift and bright,
She darted to her shallop light,

And, eagerly while Roderick scanned,
For her dear form, his mother's band,
The islet far behind her lay,
And she had landed in the bay.

XXII.

Some feelings are to mortals given
With less of earth in them than heaven;
And if there be a human tear
From passion's dross refined and clear,
A tear so limpid and so meek
It would not stain an angel's cheek,
'Tis that which pious fathers shed
Upon a duteous daughter's head!
And as the Douglas to his breast
His darling Ellen closely pressed,
Such holy drops her tresses steeped,
Though 't was an hero's eye that weeped.
Nor while on Ellen's faltering tongue
Her filial welcomes crowded hung,
Marked she that fear--affection's proof--
Still held a graceful youth aloof;
No! not till Douglas named his name,
Although the youth was Malcolm Graeme.

XXIII.

Allan, with wistful look the while,
Marked Roderick landing on the isle;
His master piteously he eyed,
Then gazed upon the Chieftain's pride,
Then dashed with hasty hand away
From his dimmed eye the gathering spray;
And Douglas, as his hand he laid
On Malcolm's shoulder, kindly said:
'Canst thou, young friend, no meaning spy
In my poor follower's glistening eye?
I 'll tell thee:--he recalls the day
When in my praise he led the lay
O'er the arched gate of Bothwell proud,

While many a minstrel answered loud,
When Percy's Norman pennon, won
In bloody field, before me shone,
And twice ten knights, the least a name
As mighty as yon Chief may claim,
Gracing my pomp, behind me came.
Yet trust me, Malcolm, not so proud
Was I of all that marshalled crowd,
Though the waned crescent owned my might,
And in my train trooped lord and knight,
Though Blantyre hymned her holiest lays,
And Bothwell's bards flung back my praise,
As when this old man's silent tear,
And this poor maid's affection dear,
A welcome give more kind and true
Than aught my better fortunes knew.
Forgive, my friend, a father's boast,--
O, it out-beggars all I lost!'

XXIV.

Delightful praise!--like summer rose,
That brighter in the dew-drop glows,
The bashful maiden's cheek appeared,
For Douglas spoke, and Malcolm heard.
The flush of shame-faced joy to hide,
The hounds, the hawk, her cares divide;
The loved caresses of the maid
The dogs with crouch and whimper paid;
And, at her whistle, on her hand
The falcon took his favorite stand,
Closed his dark wing, relaxed his eye,
Nor, though unhooded, sought to fly.
And, trust, while in such guise she stood,
Like fabled Goddess of the wood,
That if a father's partial thought
O'erweighed her worth and beauty aught,
Well might the lover's judgment fail
To balance with a juster scale;
For with each secret glance he stole,
The fond enthusiast sent his soul.

XXV.

Of stature fair, and slender frame,
But firmly knit, was Malcolm Graeme.
The belted plaid and tartan hose
Did ne'er more graceful limbs disclose;
His flaxen hair, of sunny hue,
Curled closely round his bonnet blue.
Trained to the chase, his eagle eye
The ptarmigan in snow could spy;
Each pass, by mountain, lake, and heath,
He knew, through Lennox and Menteith;
Vain was the bound of dark-brown doe
When Malcolm bent his sounding bow,
And scarce that doe, though winged with fear,
Outstripped in speed the mountaineer:
Right up Ben Lomond could he press,
And not a sob his toil confess.
His form accorded with a mind
Lively and ardent, frank and kind;
A blither heart, till Ellen came
Did never love nor sorrow tame;
It danced as lightsome in his breast
As played the feather on his crest.
Yet friends, who nearest knew the youth
His scorn of wrong, his zeal for truth
And bards, who saw his features bold
When kindled by the tales of old
Said, were that youth to manhood grown,
Not long should Roderick Dhu's renown
Be foremost voiced by mountain fame,
But quail to that of Malcolm Graeme.

XXVI.

Now back they wend their watery way,
And, 'O my sire!' did Ellen say,
'Why urge thy chase so far astray?
And why so late returned? And why '--
The rest was in her speaking eye.
'My child, the chase I follow far,

'Tis mimicry of noble war;
And with that gallant pastime reft
Were all of Douglas I have left.
I met young Malcolm as I strayed
Far eastward, in Glenfinlas' shade
Nor strayed I safe, for all around
Hunters and horsemen scoured the ground.
This youth, though still a royal ward,
Risked life and land to be my guard,
And through the passes of the wood
Guided my steps, not unpursued;
And Roderick shall his welcome make,
Despite old spleen, for Douglas' sake.
Then must he seek Strath-Endrick glen
Nor peril aught for me again.'

XXVII.

Sir Roderick, who to meet them came,
Reddened at sight of Malcolm Graeme,
Yet, not in action, word, or eye,
Failed aught in hospitality.
In talk and sport they whiled away
The morning of that summer day;
But at high noon a courier light
Held secret parley with the knight,
Whose moody aspect soon declared
That evil were the news he heard.
Deep thought seemed toiling in his head;
Yet was the evening banquet made
Ere he assembled round the flame
His mother, Douglas, and the Graeme,
And Ellen too; then cast around
His eyes, then fixed them on the ground,
As studying phrase that might avail
Best to convey unpleasant tale.
Long with his dagger's hilt he played,
Then raised his haughty brow, and said:--

XXVIII.

'Short be my speech; -- nor time affords,
Nor my plain temper, glozing words.
Kinsman and father,--if such name
Douglas vouchsafe to Roderick's claim;
Mine honored mother;--Ellen,--why,
My cousin, turn away thine eye?--
And Graeme, in whom I hope to know
Full soon a noble friend or foe,
When age shall give thee thy command,
And leading in thy native land,--
List all!--The King's vindictive pride
Boasts to have tamed the Border-side,
Where chiefs, with hound and trawl; who came
To share their monarch's sylvan game,
Themselves in bloody toils were snared,
And when the banquet they prepared,
And wide their loyal portals flung,
O'er their own gateway struggling hung.
Loud cries their blood from Meggat's mead,
From Yarrow braes and banks of Tweed,
Where the lone streams of Ettrick glide,
And from the silver Teviot's side;
The dales, where martial clans did ride,
Are now one sheep-walk, waste and wide.
This tyrant of the Scottish throne,
So faithless and so ruthless known,
Now hither comes; his end the same,
The same pretext of sylvan game.
What grace for Highland Chiefs, judge ye
By fate of Border chivalry.
Yet more; amid Glenfinlas' green,
Douglas, thy stately form was seen.
This by espial sure I know:
Your counsel in the streight I show.'

XXIX.

Ellen and Margaret fearfully
Sought comfort in each other's eye,
Then turned their ghastly look, each one,
This to her sire, that to her son.
The hasty color went and came

In the bold cheek of Malcohm Graeme,
But from his glance it well appeared
'T was but for Ellen that he feared;
While, sorrowful, but undismayed,
The Douglas thus his counsel said:
'Brave Roderick, though the tempest roar,
It may but thunder and pass o'er;
Nor will I here remain an hour,
To draw the lightning on thy bower;
For well thou know'st, at this gray head
The royal bolt were fiercest sped.
For thee, who, at thy King's command,
Canst aid him with a gallant band,
Submission, homage, humbled pride,
Shall turn the Monarch's wrath aside.
Poor remnants of the Bleeding Heart,
Ellen and I will seek apart
The refuge of some forest cell,
There, like the hunted quarry, dwell,
Till on the mountain and the moor
The stern pursuit be passed and o'er,'--

XXX.

'No, by mine honor,' Roderick said,
'So help me Heaven, and my good blade!
No, never! Blasted be yon Pine,
My father's ancient crest and mine,
If from its shade in danger part
The lineage of the Bleeding Heart!
Hear my blunt speech: grant me this maid
To wife, thy counsel to mine aid;
To Douglas, leagued with Roderick Dhu,
Will friends and allies flock enow;
Like cause of doubt, distrust, and grief,
Will bind to us each Western Chief
When the loud pipes my bridal tell,
The Links of Forth shall hear the knell,
The guards shall start in Stirling's porch;
And when I light the nuptial torch,
A thousand villages in flames
Shall scare the slumbers of King James!--

Nay, Ellen, blench not thus away,
And, mother, cease these signs, I pray;
I meant not all my heat might say.--
Small need of inroad or of fight,
When the sage Douglas may unite
Each mountain clan in friendly band,
To guard the passes of their land,
Till the foiled King from pathless glen
Shall bootless turn him home again.'

XXXI.

There are who have, at midnight hour,
In slumber scaled a dizzy tower,
And, on the verge that beetled o'er
The ocean tide's incessant roar,
Dreamed calmly out their dangerous dream,
Till wakened by the morning beam;
When, dazzled by the eastern glow,
Such startler cast his glance below,
And saw unmeasured depth around,
And heard unintermitted sound,
And thought the battled fence so frail,
It waved like cobweb in the gale;
Amid his senses' giddy wheel,
Did he not desperate impulse feel,
Headlong to plunge himself below,
And meet the worst his fears foreshow?--
Thus Ellen, dizzy and astound,
As sudden ruin yawned around,
By crossing terrors wildly tossed,
Still for the Douglas fearing most,
Could scarce the desperate thought withstand,
To buy his safety with her hand.

XXXII.

Such purpose dread could Malcolm spy
In Ellen's quivering lip and eye,
And eager rose to speak,--but ere
His tongue could hurry forth his fear,

Had Douglas marked the hectic strife,
Where death seemed combating with life;
For to her cheek, in feverish flood,
One instant rushed the throbbing blood,
Then ebbing back, with sudden sway,
Left its domain as wan as clay.
'Roderick, enough! enough!' he cried,
'My daughter cannot be thy bride;
Not that the blush to wooer dear,
Nor paleness that of maiden fear.
It may not be,--forgive her,
Chief, Nor hazard aught for our relief.
Against his sovereign, Douglas ne'er
Will level a rebellious spear.
'T was I that taught his youthful hand
To rein a steed and wield a brand;
I see him yet, the princely boy!
Not Ellen more my pride and joy;
I love him still, despite my wrongs
By hasty wrath and slanderous tongues.
O. seek the grace you well may find,
Without a cause to mine combined!'

XXXIII.

Twice through the hall the Chieftain strode;
The waving of his tartars broad,
And darkened brow, where wounded pride
With ire and disappointment vied
Seemed, by the torch's gloomy light,
Like the ill Demon of the night,
Stooping his pinions' shadowy sway
Upon the righted pilgrim's way:
But, unrequited Love! thy dart
Plunged deepest its envenomed smart,
And Roderick, with thine anguish stung,
At length the hand of Douglas wrung,
While eyes that mocked at tears before
With bitter drops were running o'er.
The death-pangs of long-cherished hope
Scarce in that ample breast had scope
But, struggling with his spirit proud,

Convulsive heaved its checkered shroud,
While every sob--so mute were all
Was heard distinctly through the ball.
The son's despair, the mother's look,
III might the gentle Ellen brook;
She rose, and to her side there came,
To aid her parting steps, the Graeme.

XXXIV.

Then Roderick from the Douglas broke--
As flashes flame through sable smoke,
Kindling its wreaths, long, dark, and low,
To one broad blaze of ruddy glow,
So the deep anguish of despair
Burst, in fierce jealousy, to air.
With stalwart grasp his hand he laid
On Malcolm's breast and belted plaid:
'Back, beardless boy!' he sternly said,
'Back, minion! holdst thou thus at naught
The lesson I so lately taught?
This roof, the Douglas. and that maid,
Thank thou for punishment delayed.'
Eager as greyhound on his game,
Fiercely with Roderick grappled Graeme.
'Perish my name, if aught afford
Its Chieftain safety save his sword!'
Thus as they strove their desperate hand
Griped to the dagger or the brand,
And death had been--but Douglas rose,
And thrust between the struggling foes
His giant strength:--' Chieftains, forego!
I hold the first who strikes my foe.--
Madmen, forbear your frantic jar!
What! is the Douglas fallen so far,
His daughter's hand is deemed the spoil
Of such dishonorable broil?'
Sullen and slowly they unclasp,
As struck with shame, their desperate grasp,
And each upon his rival glared,
With foot advanced and blade half bared.

XXXV.

Ere yet the brands aloft were flung,
Margaret on Roderick's mantle hung,
And Malcolm heard his Ellen's scream,
As faltered through terrific dream.
Then Roderick plunged in sheath his sword,
And veiled his wrath in scornful word:'
Rest safe till morning; pity 't were
Such cheek should feel the midnight air!
Then mayst thou to James Stuart tell,
Roderick will keep the lake and fell,
Nor lackey with his freeborn clan
The pageant pomp of earthly man.
More would he of Clan-Alpine know,
Thou canst our strength and passes show.--
Malise, what ho!'--his henchman came:
'Give our safe-conduct to the Graeme.'
Young Malcolm answered, calm and bold:'
Fear nothing for thy favorite hold;
The spot an angel deigned to grace
Is blessed, though robbers haunt the place.
Thy churlish courtesy for those
Reserve, who fear to be thy foes.
As safe to me the mountain way
At midnight as in blaze of day,
Though with his boldest at his back
Even Roderick Dhu beset the track.--
Brave Douglas,--lovely Ellen,--nay,
Naught here of parting will I say.
Earth does not hold a lonesome glen
So secret but we meet again.--
Chieftain! we too shall find an hour,'--
He said, and left the sylvan bower.

XXXVI.

Old Allan followed to the strand --
Such was the Douglas's command--
And anxious told, how, on the morn,
The stern Sir Roderick deep had sworn,

The Fiery Cross should circle o'er
Dale, glen, and valley, down and moor
Much were the peril to the Graeme
From those who to the signal came;
Far up the lake 't were safest land,
Himself would row him to the strand.
He gave his counsel to the wind,
While Malcolm did, unheeding, bind,
Round dirk and pouch and broadsword rolled,
His ample plaid in tightened fold,
And stripped his limbs to such array
As best might suit the watery way,--

XXXVII.

Then spoke abrupt: 'Farewell to thee,
Pattern of old fidelity!'
The Minstrel's hand he kindly pressed,--
'O, could I point a place of rest!
My sovereign holds in ward my land,
My uncle leads my vassal band;
To tame his foes, his friends to aid,
Poor Malcolm has but heart and blade.
Yet, if there be one faithful Graeme
Who loves the chieftain of his name,
Not long shall honored Douglas dwell
Like hunted stag in mountain cell;
Nor, ere yon pride-swollen robber dare,--
I may not give the rest to air!
Tell Roderick Dhu I owed him naught,
Not tile poor service of a boat,
To waft me to yon mountain-side.'
Then plunged he in the flashing tide.
Bold o'er the flood his head he bore,
And stoutly steered him from the shore;
And Allan strained his anxious eye,
Far mid the lake his form to spy,
Darkening across each puny wave,
To which the moon her silver gave.
Fast as the cormorant could skim.
The swimmer plied each active limb;
Then landing in the moonlight dell,

Loud shouted of his weal to tell.
The Minstrel heard the far halloo,
And joyful from the shore withdrew.

The Lady of the Lake

CANTO THIRD.

The Gathering.

I.

Time rolls his ceaseless course. The race of yore,
Who danced our infancy upon their knee,
And told our marvelling boyhood legends store
Of their strange ventures happed by land or sea,
How are they blotted from the things that be!
How few, all weak and withered of their force,
Wait on the verge of dark eternity,
Like stranded wrecks, the tide returning hoarse,
To sweep them from out sight! Time rolls his ceaseless course.

Yet live there still who can remember well,
How, when a mountain chief his bugle blew,
Both field and forest, dingle, cliff; and dell,
And solitary heath, the signal knew;
And fast the faithful clan around him drew.
What time the warning note was keenly wound,
What time aloft their kindred banner flew,
While clamorous war-pipes yelled the gathering sound,
And while the Fiery Cross glanced like a meteor, round.

II.

The Summer dawn's reflected hue
To purple changed Loch Katrine blue;
Mildly and soft the western breeze
Just kissed the lake, just stirred the trees,
And the pleased lake, like maiden coy,
Trembled but dimpled not for joy
The mountain-shadows on her breast
Were neither broken nor at rest;
In bright uncertainty they lie,
Like future joys to Fancy's eye.
The water-lily to the light
Her chalice reared of silver bright;

The doe awoke, and to the lawn,
Begemmed with dew-drops, led her fawn;
The gray mist left the mountain-side,
The torrent showed its glistening pride;
Invisible in flecked sky The lark sent clown her revelry:
The blackbird and the speckled thrush
Good-morrow gave from brake and bush;
In answer cooed the cushat dove
Her notes of peace and rest and love.

III.

No thought of peace, no thought of rest,
Assuaged the storm in Roderick's breast.
With sheathed broadsword in his hand,
Abrupt he paced the islet strand,
And eyed the rising sun, and laid
His hand on his impatient blade.
Beneath a rock, his vassals' care
Was prompt the ritual to prepare,
With deep and deathful meaning fraught;
For such Antiquity had taught
Was preface meet, ere yet abroad
The Cross of Fire should take its road.
The shrinking band stood oft aghast
At the impatient glance he cast;--
Such glance the mountain eagle threw,
As, from the cliffs of Benvenue,
She spread her dark sails on the wind,
And, high in middle heaven reclined,
With her broad shadow on the lake,
Silenced the warblers of the brake.

IV.

A heap of withered boughs was piled,
Of juniper and rowan wild,
Mingled with shivers from the oak,
Rent by the lightning's recent stroke.
Brian the Hermit by it stood,
Barefooted, in his frock and hood.

His grizzled beard and matted hair
Obscured a visage of despair;
His naked arms and legs, seamed o'er,
The scars of frantic penance bore.
That monk, of savage form and face
The impending danger of his race
Had drawn from deepest solitude
Far in Benharrow's bosom rude.
Not his the mien of Christian priest,
But Druid's, from the grave released
Whose hardened heart and eye might brook
On human sacrifice to look;
And much, 't was said, of heathen lore
Mixed in the charms he muttered o'er.
The hallowed creed gave only worse
And deadlier emphasis of curse.
No peasant sought that Hermit's prayer
His cave the pilgrim shunned with care,
The eager huntsman knew his bound
And in mid chase called off his hound;'
Or if, in lonely glen or strath,
The desert-dweller met his path
He prayed, and signed the cross between,
While terror took devotion's mien.

V.

Of Brian's birth strange tales were told.
His mother watched a midnight fold,
Built deep within a dreary glen,
Where scattered lay the bones of men
In some forgotten battle slain,
And bleached by drifting wind and rain.
It might have tamed a warrior's heart
To view such mockery of his art!
The knot-grass fettered there the hand
Which once could burst an iron band;
Beneath the broad and ample bone,
That bucklered heart to fear unknown,
A feeble and a timorous guest,
The fieldfare framed her lowly nest;
There the slow blindworm left his slime

On the fleet limbs that mocked at time;
And there, too, lay the leader's skull
Still wreathed with chaplet, flushed and full,
For heath-bell with her purple bloom
Supplied the bonnet and the plume.
All night, in this sad glen the maid
Sat shrouded in her mantle's shade:
She said no shepherd sought her side,
No hunter's hand her snood untied.
Yet ne'er again to braid her hair
The virgin snood did Alive wear;
Gone was her maiden glee and sport,
Her maiden girdle all too short,
Nor sought she, from that fatal night,
Or holy church or blessed rite
But locked her secret in her breast,
And died in travail, unconfessed.

VI.

Alone, among his young compeers,
Was Brian from his infant years;
A moody and heart-broken boy,
Estranged from sympathy and joy
Bearing each taunt which careless tongue
On his mysterious lineage flung.
Whole nights he spent by moonlight pale
To wood and stream his teal, to wail,
Till, frantic, he as truth received
What of his birth the crowd believed,
And sought, in mist and meteor fire,
To meet and know his Phantom Sire!
In vain, to soothe his wayward fate,
The cloister oped her pitying gate;
In vain the learning of the age
Unclasped the sable-lettered page;
Even in its treasures he could find
Food for the fever of his mind.
Eager he read whatever tells
Of magic, cabala, and spells,
And every dark pursuit allied
To curious and presumptuous pride;

Till with fired brain and nerves o'erstrung,
And heart with mystic horrors wrung,
Desperate he sought Benharrow's den,
And hid him from the haunts of men.

VII.

The desert gave him visions wild,
Such as might suit the spectre's child.
Where with black cliffs the torrents toil,
He watched the wheeling eddies boil,
Jill from their foam his dazzled eyes
Beheld the River Demon rise:
The mountain mist took form and limb
Of noontide hag or goblin grim;
The midnight wind came wild and dread,
Swelled with the voices of the dead;
Far on the future battle-heath
His eye beheld the ranks of death:
Thus the lone Seer, from mankind hurled,
Shaped forth a disembodied world.
One lingering sympathy of mind
Still bound him to the mortal kind;
The only parent he could claim
Of ancient Alpine's lineage came.
Late had he heard, in prophet's dream,
The fatal Ben-Shie's boding scream;
Sounds, too, had come in midnight blast
Of charging steeds, careering fast
Along Benharrow's shingly side,
Where mortal horseman ne'er might ride;
The thunderbolt had split the pine,--
All augured ill to Alpine's line.
He girt his loins, and came to show
The signals of impending woe,
And now stood prompt to bless or ban,
As bade the Chieftain of his clan.

VIII.

'T was all prepared;--and from the rock

A goat, the patriarch of the flock,
Before the kindling pile was laid,
And pierced by Roderick's ready blade.
Patient the sickening victim eyed
The life-blood ebb in crimson tide
Down his clogged beard and shaggy limb,
Till darkness glazed his eyeballs dim.
The grisly priest, with murmuring prayer,
A slender crosslet framed with care,
A cubit's length in measure due;
The shaft and limbs were rods of yew,
Whose parents in Inch-Cailliach wave
Their shadows o'er Clan-Alpine's grave,
And, answering Lomond's breezes deep,
Soothe many a chieftain's endless sleep.
The Cross thus formed he held on high,
With wasted hand and haggard eye,
And strange and mingled feelings woke,
While his anathema he spoke:--

IX.

'Woe to the clansman who shall view
This symbol of sepulchral yew,
Forgetful that its branches grew
Where weep the heavens their holiest dew
On Alpine's dwelling low!
Deserter of his Chieftain's trust,
He ne'er shall mingle with their dust,
But, from his sires and kindred thrust,
Each clansman's execration just
Shall doom him wrath and woe.'
He paused; -- the word the vassals took,
With forward step and fiery look,
On high their naked brands they shook,
Their clattering targets wildly strook;
And first in murmur low,
Then like the billow in his course,
That far to seaward finds his source,
And flings to shore his mustered force,
Burst with loud roar their answer hoarse,
'Woe to the traitor, woe!'

Ben-an's gray scalp the accents knew,
The joyous wolf from covert drew,
The exulting eagle screamed afar,--
They knew the voice of Alpine's war.

X.

The shout was hushed on lake and fell,
The Monk resumed his muttered spell:
Dismal and low its accents came,
The while he scathed the Cross with flame;
And the few words that reached the air,
Although the holiest name was there,
Had more of blasphemy than prayer.
But when he shook above the crowd
Its kindled points, he spoke aloud:--
'Woe to the wretch who fails to rear
At this dread sign the ready spear!
For, as the flames this symbol sear,
His home, the refuge of his fear,
A kindred fate shall know;
Far o'er its roof the volumed flame
Clan-Alpine's vengeance shall proclaim,
While maids and matrons on his name
Shall call down wretchedness and shame,
And infamy and woe.'
Then rose the cry of females, shrill
As goshawk's whistle on the hill,
Denouncing misery and ill,
Mingled with childhood's babbling trill
Of curses stammered slow;
Answering with imprecation dread,
'Sunk be his home in embers red!
And cursed be the meanest shed
That o'er shall hide the houseless head
We doom to want and woe!'
A sharp and shrieking echo gave,
Coir-Uriskin, thy goblin cave!
And the gray pass where birches wave
On Beala-nam-bo.

XI.

Then deeper paused the priest anew,
And hard his laboring breath he drew,
While, with set teeth and clenched hand,
And eyes that glowed like fiery brand,
He meditated curse more dread,
And deadlier, on the clansman's head
Who, summoned to his chieftain's aid,
The signal saw and disobeyed.
The crosslet's points of sparkling wood
He quenched among the bubbling blood.
And, as again the sign he reared,
Hollow and hoarse his voice was heard:
'When flits this Cross from man to man,
Vich-Alpine's summons to his clan,
Burst be the ear that fails to heed!
Palsied the foot that shuns to speed!
May ravens tear the careless eyes,
Wolves make the coward heart their prize!
As sinks that blood-stream in the earth,
So may his heart's-blood drench his hearth!
As dies in hissing gore the spark,
Quench thou his light, Destruction dark!
And be the grace to him denied,
Bought by this sign to all beside!
He ceased; no echo gave again
The murmur of the deep Amen.

XII.

Then Roderick with impatient look
From Brian's hand the symbol took:
'Speed, Malise, speed' he said, and gave
The crosslet to his henchman brave.
'The muster-place be Lanrick mead--
Instant the time---speed, Malise, speed!'
Like heath-bird, when the hawks pursue,
A barge across Loch Katrine flew:
High stood the henchman on the prow;
So rapidly the barge-mall row,
The bubbles, where they launched the boat,

Were all unbroken and afloat,
Dancing in foam and ripple still,
When it had neared the mainland hill;
And from the silver beach's side
Still was the prow three fathom wide,
When lightly bounded to the land
The messenger of blood and brand.

XIII.

Speed, Malise, speed! the dun deer's hide
On fleeter foot was never tied.
Speed, Malise, speed! such cause of haste
Thine active sinews never braced.
Bend 'gainst the steepy hill thy breast,
Burst down like torrent from its crest;
With short and springing footstep pass
The trembling bog and false morass;
Across the brook like roebuck bound,
And thread the brake like questing hound;
The crag is high, the scaur is deep,
Yet shrink not from the desperate leap:
Parched are thy burning lips and brow,
Yet by the fountain pause not now;
Herald of battle, fate, and fear,
Stretch onward in thy fleet career!
The wounded hind thou track'st not now,
Pursuest not maid through greenwood bough,
Nor priest thou now thy flying pace
With rivals in the mountain race;
But danger, death, and warrior deed
Are in thy course--speed, Malise, speed!

XIV.

Fast as the fatal symbol flies,
In arms the huts and hamlets rise;
From winding glen, from upland brown,
They poured each hardy tenant down.
Nor slacked the messenger his pace;
He showed the sign, he named the place,

And, pressing forward like the wind,
Left clamor and surprise behind.
The fisherman forsook the strand,
The swarthy smith took dirk and brand;
With changed cheer, the mower blithe
Left in the half-cut swath his scythe;
The herds without a keeper strayed,
The plough was in mid-furrow staved,
The falconer tossed his hawk away,
The hunter left the stag at hay;
Prompt at the signal of alarms,
Each son of Alpine rushed to arms;
So swept the tumult and affray
Along the margin of Achray.
Alas, thou lovely lake! that e'er
Thy banks should echo sounds of fear!
The rocks, the bosky thickets, sleep
So stilly on thy bosom deep,
The lark's blithe carol from the cloud
Seems for the scene too gayly loud.

XV.

Speed, Malise, speed! The lake is past,
Duncraggan's huts appear at last,
And peep, like moss-grown rocks, half seen
Half hidden in the copse so green;
There mayst thou rest, thy labor done,
Their lord shall speed the signal on.--
As stoops the hawk upon his prey,
The henchman shot him down the way.
What woful accents load the gale?
The funeral yell, the female wail!
A gallant hunter's sport is o'er,
A valiant warrior fights no more.
Who, in the battle or the chase,
At Roderick's side shall fill his place!--
Within the hall, where torch's ray
Supplies the excluded beams of day,
Lies Duncan on his lowly bier,
And o'er him streams his widow's tear.
His stripling son stands mournful by,

His youngest weeps, but knows not why;
The village maids and matrons round
The dismal coronach resound.

XVI.

Coronach.

He is gone on the mountain,
He is lost to the forest,
Like a summer-dried fountain,
When our need was the sorest.
The font, reappearing,
From the rain-drops shall borrow,
But to us comes no cheering,
To Duncan no morrow!

The hand of the reaper
Takes the ears that are hoary,
But the voice of the weeper
Wails manhood in glory.
The autumn winds rushing
Waft the leaves that are searest,
But our flower was in flushing,
When blighting was nearest.

Fleet foot on the correi,
Sage counsel in cumber,
Red hand in the foray,
How sound is thy slumber!
Like the dew on the mountain,
Like the foam on the river,
Like the bubble on the fountain,
Thou art gone, and forever!

XVII.

See Stumah, who, the bier beside
His master's corpse with wonder eyed,
Poor Stumah! whom his least halloo
Could send like lightning o'er the dew,

Bristles his crest, and points his ears,
As if some stranger step he hears.
'T is not a mourner's muffled tread,
Who comes to sorrow o'er the dead,
But headlong haste or deadly fear
Urge the precipitate career.
All stand aghast:--unheeding all,
The henchman bursts into the hall;
Before the dead man's bier he stood,
Held forth the Cross besmeared with blood;
'The muster-place is Lanrick mead;
Speed forth the signal! clansmen, speed!'

XVIII,

Angus, the heir of Duncan's line,
Sprung forth and seized the fatal sign.
In haste the stripling to his side
His father's dirk and broadsword tied;
But when he saw his mother's eye
Watch him in speechless agony,
Back to her opened arms he flew
Pressed on her lips a fond adieu,--
'Alas' she sobbed,--'and yet be gone,
And speed thee forth, like Duncan's son!'
One look he cast upon the bier,
Dashed from his eye the gathering tear,
Breathed deep to clear his laboring breast,
And tossed aloft his bonnet crest,
Then, like the high-bred colt when, freed,
First he essays his fire and speed,
He vanished, and o'er moor and moss
Sped forward with the Fiery Cross.
Suspended was the widow's tear
While yet his footsteps she could hear;
And when she marked the henchman's eye
Wet with unwonted sympathy,
'Kinsman,' she said, 'his race is run
That should have sped thine errand on.
The oak teas fallen?--the sapling bough Is all
Duncraggan's shelter now
Yet trust I well, his duty done,

The orphan's God will guard my son.--
And you, in many a danger true
At Duncan's hest your blades that drew,
To arms, and guard that orphan's head!
Let babes and women wail the dead.'
Then weapon-clang and martial call
Resounded through the funeral hall,
While from the walls the attendant band
Snatched sword and targe with hurried hand;
And short and flitting energy
Glanced from the mourner's sunken eye,
As if the sounds to warrior dear
Might rouse her Duncan from his bier.
But faded soon that borrowed force;
Grief claimed his right, and tears their course.

XIX.

Benledi saw the Cross of Fire,
It glanced like lightning up Strath-Ire.
O'er dale and hill the summons flew,
Nor rest nor pause young Angus knew;
The tear that gathered in his eye
He deft the mountain-breeze to dry;
Until, where Teith's young waters roll
Betwixt him and a wooded knoll
That graced the sable strath with green,
The chapel of Saint Bride was seen.
Swoln was the stream, remote the bridge,
But Angus paused not on the edge;
Though the clerk waves danced dizzily,
Though reeled his sympathetic eye,
He dashed amid the torrent's roar:
His right hand high the crosslet bore,
His left the pole-axe grasped, to guide
And stay his footing in the tide.
He stumbled twice,--the foam splashed high,
With hoarser swell the stream raced by;
And had he fallen,--forever there,
Farewell Duncraggan's orphan heir!
But still, as if in parting life,
Firmer he grasped the Cross of strife,

Until the opposing bank he gained,
And up the chapel pathway strained.
A blithesome rout that morning-tide
Had sought the chapel of Saint Bride.
Her troth Tombea's Mary gave
To Norman, heir of Armandave,
And, issuing from the Gothic arch,
The bridal now resumed their march.
In rude but glad procession came
Bonneted sire and coif-clad dame;
And plaided youth, with jest and jeer
Which snooded maiden would not hear:
And children, that, unwitting why,
Lent the gay shout their shrilly cry;
And minstrels, that in measures vied
Before the young and bonny bride,
Whose downcast eye and cheek disclose
The tear and blush of morning rose.
With virgin step and bashful hand
She held the kerchief's snowy band.
The gallant bridegroom by her side
Beheld his prize with victor's pride.
And the glad mother in her ear
Was closely whispering word of cheer.

XXI.

Who meets them at the churchyard gate?
The messenger of fear and fate!
Haste in his hurried accent lies,
And grief is swimming in his eyes.
All dripping from the recent flood,
Panting and travel-soiled he stood,
The fatal sign of fire and sword
Held forth, and spoke the appointed word:
'The muster-place is Lanrick mead;
Speed forth the signal! Norman, speed!'
And must he change so soon the hand
Just linked to his by holy band,
For the fell Cross of blood and brand?
And must the day so blithe that rose,
And promised rapture in the close,

Before its setting hour, divide
The bridegroom from the plighted bride?
O fatal doom'--it must! it must!
Clan-Alpine's cause, her Chieftain's trust,
Her summons dread, brook no delay;
Stretch to the race,--away! away!

XXII.

Yet slow he laid his plaid aside,
And lingering eyed his lovely bride,
Until he saw the starting tear
Speak woe he might not stop to cheer:
Then, trusting not a second look,
In haste he sped hind up the brook,
Nor backward glanced till on the heath
Where Lubnaig's lake supplies the Teith,--
What in the racer's bosom stirred?
The sickening pang of hope deferred,
And memory with a torturing train
Of all his morning visions vain.
Mingled with love's impatience, came
The manly thirst for martial fame;
The stormy joy of mountaineers
Ere yet they rush upon the spears;
And zeal for Clan and Chieftain burning,
And hope, from well-fought field returning,
With war's red honors on his crest,
To clasp his Mary to his breast.
Stung by such thoughts, o'er bank and brae,
Like fire from flint he glanced away,
While high resolve and feeling strong
Burst into voluntary song.

XXIII.

Song.

The heath this night must be my bed,
The bracken curtain for my head,
My lullaby the warder's tread,

Far, far, from love and thee, Mary;
To-morrow eve, more stilly laid,
My couch may be my bloody plaid,
My vesper song thy wail, sweet maid!
It will not waken me, Mary!

I may not, dare not, fancy now
The grief that clouds thy lovely brow,
I dare not think upon thy vow,
And all it promised me, Mary.
No fond regret must Norman know;
When bursts Clan-Alpine on the foe,
His heart must be like bended bow,
His foot like arrow free, Mary.

A time will come with feeling fraught,
For, if I fall in battle fought,
Thy hapless lover's dying thought
Shall be a thought on thee, Mary.
And if returned from conquered foes,
How blithely will the evening close,
How sweet the linnet sing repose,
To my young bride and me, Mary!

XXIV.

Not faster o'er thy heathery braes
Balquidder, speeds the midnight blaze,
Rushing in conflagration strong
Thy deep ravines and dells along,
Wrapping thy cliffs in purple glow,
And reddening the dark lakes below;
Nor faster speeds it, nor so far,
As o'er thy heaths the voice of war.
The signal roused to martial coil
The sullen margin of Loch Voil,
Waked still Loch Doine, and to the source
Alarmed, Balvaig, thy swampy course;
Thence southward turned its rapid road
Adown Strath-Gartney's valley broad
Till rose in arms each man might claim
A portion in Clan-Alpine's name,

From the gray sire, whose trembling hand
Could hardly buckle on his brand,
To the raw boy, whose shaft and bow
Were yet scarce terror to the crow.
Each valley, each sequestered glen,
Mustered its little horde of men
That met as torrents from the height
In Highland dales their streams unite
Still gathering, as they pour along,
A voice more loud, a tide more strong,
Till at the rendezvous they stood
By hundreds prompt for blows and blood,
Each trained to arms since life began,
Owning no tie but to his clan,
No oath but by his chieftain's hand,
No law but Roderick Dhu's command.

XXV.

That summer morn had Roderick Dhu
Surveyed the skirts of Benvenue,
And sent his scouts o'er hill and heath,
To view the frontiers of Menteith.
All backward came with news of truce;
Still lay each martial Graeme and Bruce,
In Rednock courts no horsemen wait,
No banner waved on Cardross gate,
On Duchray's towers no beacon shone,
Nor scared the herons from Loch Con;
All seemed at peace.--Now wot ye wily
The Chieftain with such anxious eye,
Ere to the muster he repair,
This western frontier scanned with care?--
In Benvenue's most darksome cleft,
A fair though cruel pledge was left;
For Douglas, to his promise true,
That morning from the isle withdrew,
And in a deep sequestered dell
Had sought a low and lonely cell.
By many a bard in Celtic tongue
Has Coir-nan-Uriskin been sung
A softer name the Saxons gave,

And called the grot the Goblin Cave.

XXVI.

It was a wild and strange retreat,
As e'er was trod by outlaw's feet.
The dell, upon the mountain's crest,
Yawned like a gash on warrior's breast;
Its trench had stayed full many a rock,
Hurled by primeval earthquake shock
From Benvenue's gray summit wild,
And here, in random ruin piled,
They frowned incumbent o'er the spot
And formed the rugged sylvan "rot.
The oak and birch with mingled shade
At noontide there a twilight made,
Unless when short and sudden shone
Some straggling beam on cliff or stone,
With such a glimpse as prophet's eye
Gains on thy depth, Futurity.
No murmur waked the solemn still,
Save tinkling of a fountain rill;
But when the wind chafed with the lake,
A sullen sound would upward break,
With dashing hollow voice, that spoke
The incessant war of wave and rock.
Suspended cliffs with hideous sway
Seemed nodding o'er the cavern gray.
From such a den the wolf had sprung,
In such the wild-cat leaves her young;
Yet Douglas and his daughter fair
Sought for a space their safety there.
Gray Superstition's whisper dread
Debarred the spot to vulgar tread;
For there, she said, did fays resort,
And satyrs hold their sylvan court,
By moonlight tread their mystic maze,
And blast the rash beholder's gaze.

XXVII.

Now eve, with western shadows long,
Floated on Katrine bright and strong,
When Roderick with a chosen few
Repassed the heights of Benvenue.
Above the Goblin Cave they go,
Through the wild pass of Beal-nam-bo;
The prompt retainers speed before,
To launch the shallop from the shore,
For 'cross Loch Katrine lies his way
To view the passes of Achray,
And place his clansmen in array.
Yet lags the Chief in musing mind,
Unwonted sight, his men behind.
A single page, to bear his sword,
Alone attended on his lord;
The rest their way through thickets break,
And soon await him by the lake.
It was a fair and gallant sight
To view them from the neighboring height,
By the low-levelled sunbeam's light!
For strength and stature, from the clan
Each warrior was a chosen man,
As even afar might well be seen,
By their proud step and martial mien.
heir feathers dance, their tartars float,
Their targets gleam, as by the boat
A wild and warlike group they stand,
That well became such mountain-strand.

XXVI

Their Chief with step reluctant still
Was lingering on the craggy hill,
Hard by where turned apart the road
To Douglas's obscure abode.
It was but with that dawning morn
That Roderick Dhu had proudly sworn
To drown his love in war's wild roar,
Nor think of Ellen Douglas more;
But he who stems a stream with sand,
And fetters flame with flaxen band,
Has yet a harder task to prove,--

By firm resolve to conquer love!
Eve finds the Chief, like restless ghost,
Still hovering near his treasure lost;
For though his haughty heart deny
A parting meeting to his eye
Still fondly strains his anxious ear
The accents of her voice to hear,
And inly did he curse the breeze
That waked to sound the rustling trees.
But hark! what mingles in the strain?
It is the harp of Allan-bane,
That wakes its measure slow and high,
Attuned to sacred minstrelsy.
What melting voice attends the strings?
'Tis Ellen, or an angel, sings.

XXIX.

Hymn to the Virgin.

Ave. Maria! maiden mild!
Listen to a maiden's prayer!
Thou canst hear though from the wild,
Thou canst save amid despair.
Safe may we sleep beneath thy care,
Though banished, outcast, and reviled--
Maiden! hear a maiden's prayer;
Mother, hear a suppliant child!
Ave Maria!

Ave Maria! undefiled!
The flinty couch we now must share
Shall seem with down of eider piled,
If thy protection hover there.
The murky cavern's heavy air
Shall breathe of balm if thou hast smiled;
Then, Maiden! hear a maiden's prayer,
Mother, list a suppliant child!
Ave Maria!

Ave. Maria! stainless styled!
Foul demons of the earth and air,

From this their wonted haunt exiled,
Shall flee before thy presence fair.
We bow us to our lot of care,
Beneath thy guidance reconciled:
Hear for a maid a maiden's prayer,
And for a father hear a child!
Ave Maria!

XXX.

Died on the harp the closing hymn,--
Unmoved in attitude and limb,
As listening still, Clan-Alpine's lord
Stood leaning on his heavy sword,
Until the page with humble sign
Twice pointed to the sun's decline.
Then while his plaid he round him cast,
'It is the last time--'tis the last,'
He muttered thrice,--'the last time e'er
That angel-voice shall Roderick hear''
It was a goading thought,--his stride
Hied hastier down the mountain-side;
Sullen he flung him in the boat
An instant 'cross the lake it shot.
They landed in that silvery bay,
And eastward held their hasty way
Till, with the latest beams of light,
The band arrived on Lanrick height'
Where mustered in the vale below
Clan-Alpine's men in martial show.

XXXI.

A various scene the clansmen made:
Some sat, some stood, some slowly strayer):
But most, with mantles folded round,
Were couched to rest upon the ground,
Scarce to be known by curious eye
From the deep heather where they lie,
So well was matched the tartan screen
With heath-bell dark and brackens green;

Unless where, here and there, a blade
Or lance's point a glimmer made,
Like glow-worm twinkling through the shade.
But when, advancing through the gloom,
They saw the Chieftain's eagle plume,
Their shout of welcome, shrill and wide,
Shook the steep mountain's steady side.
Thrice it arose, and lake and fell
Three times returned the martial yell;
It died upon Bochastle's plain,
And Silence claimed her evening reign.

The Lady of the Lake

CANTO FOURTH.

The Prophecy.

I.

The rose is fairest when 't is budding new,
And hope is brightest when it dawns from fears;
The rose is sweetest washed with morning dew
And love is loveliest when embalmed in tears.
O wilding rose, whom fancy thus endears,
I bid your blossoms in my bonnet wave,
Emblem of hope and love through future years!'
Thus spoke young Norman, heir of Armandave,
What time the sun arose on Vennachar's broad wave.

II.

Such fond conceit, half said, half sung,
Love prompted to the bridegroom's tongue.
All while he stripped the wild-rose spray,
His axe and bow beside him lay,
For on a pass 'twixt lake and wood
A wakeful sentinel he stood.
Hark!--on the rock a footstep rung,
And instant to his arms he sprung.
'Stand, or thou diest!--What, Malise?--soon
Art thou returned from Braes of Doune.
By thy keen step and glance I know,
Thou bring'st us tidings of the foe.'--
For while the Fiery Cross tried on,
On distant scout had Malise gone.--
'Where sleeps the Chief?' the henchman said.
'Apart, in yonder misty glade;
To his lone couch I'll be your guide.'--
Then called a slumberer by his side,
And stirred him with his slackened bow,--
'Up, up, Glentarkin! rouse thee, ho!
We seek the Chieftain; on the track
Keep eagle watch till I come back.'

III.

Together up the pass they sped:
'What of the foeman?' Norman said.--
'Varying reports from near and far;
This certain,--that a band of war
Has for two days been ready boune,
At prompt command to march from Doune;
King James the while, with princely powers,
Holds revelry in Stirling towers.
Soon will this dark and gathering cloud
Speak on our glens in thunder loud.
Inured to bide such bitter bout,
The warrior's plaid may bear it out;
But, Norman, how wilt thou provide
A shelter for thy bonny bride?"--
'What! know ye not that Roderick's care
To the lone isle hath caused repair
Each maid and matron of the clan,
And every child and aged man
Unfit for arms; and given his charge,
Nor skiff nor shallop, boat nor barge,
Upon these lakes shall float at large,
But all beside the islet moor,
That such dear pledge may rest secure?'--

IV.

' 'T is well advised,--the Chieftain's plan
Bespeaks the father of his clan.
But wherefore sleeps Sir Roderick Dhu
Apart from all his followers true?'
'It is because last evening-tide
Brian an augury hath tried,
Of that dread kind which must not be
Unless in dread extremity,
The Taghairm called; by which, afar,
Our sires foresaw the events of war.
Duncraggan's milk-white bull they slew,'--

Malise.

'Ah! well the gallant brute I knew!
The choicest of the prey we had
When swept our merrymen Gallangad.
His hide was snow, his horns were dark,
His red eye glowed like fiery spark;
So fierce, so tameless, and so fleet,
Sore did he cumber our retreat,
And kept our stoutest kerns in awe,
Even at the pass of Beal 'maha.
But steep and flinty was the road,
And sharp the hurrying pikeman's goad,
And when we came to Dennan's Row
A child might scathless stroke his brow.'

V.

Norman.

'That bull was slain; his reeking hide
They stretched the cataract beside,
Whose waters their wild tumult toss
Adown the black and craggy boss
Of that huge cliff whose ample verge
Tradition calls the Hero's Targe.
Couched on a shelf beneath its brink,
Close where the thundering torrents sink,
Rocking beneath their headlong sway,
And drizzled by the ceaseless spray,
Midst groan of rock and roar of stream,
The wizard waits prophetic dream.
Nor distant rests the Chief;--but hush!
See, gliding slow through mist and bush,
The hermit gains yon rock, and stands
To gaze upon our slumbering bands.
Seems he not, Malise, dike a ghost,
That hovers o'er a slaughtered host?
Or raven on the blasted oak,
That, watching while the deer is broke,
His morsel claims with sullen croak?'

Malise.

'Peace! peace! to other than to me
Thy words were evil augury;
But still I hold Sir Roderick's blade
Clan-Alpine's omen and her aid,
Not aught that, gleaned from heaven or hell,
Yon fiend-begotten Monk can tell.
The Chieftain joins him, see--and now
Together they descend the brow.'

VI.

And, as they came, with Alpine's Lord
The Hermit Monk held solemn word:--.
'Roderick! it is a fearful strife,
For man endowed with mortal life
Whose shroud of sentient clay can still
Feel feverish pang and fainting chill,
Whose eye can stare in stony trance
Whose hair can rouse like warrior's lance,
'Tis hard for such to view, unfurled,
The curtain of the future world.
Yet, witness every quaking limb,
My sunken pulse, mine eyeballs dim,
My soul with harrowing anguish torn,
This for my Chieftain have I borne!--
The shapes that sought my fearful couch
A human tongue may ne'er avouch;
No mortal man--save he, who, bred
Between the living and the dead,
Is gifted beyond nature's law
Had e'er survived to say he saw.
At length the fateful answer came
In characters of living flame!
Not spoke in word, nor blazed in scroll,
But borne and branded on my soul:--
WHICH SPILLS THE FOREMOST FOEMAN'S LIFE,
THAT PARTY CONQUERS IN THE STRIFE.'

VII.

'Thanks, Brian, for thy zeal and care!
Good is thine augury, and fair.
Clan-Alpine ne'er in battle stood
But first our broadswords tasted blood.
A surer victim still I know,
Self-offered to the auspicious blow:
A spy has sought my land this morn,--
No eve shall witness his return!
My followers guard each pass's mouth,
To east, to westward, and to south;
Red Murdoch, bribed to be his guide,
Has charge to lead his steps aside,
Till in deep path or dingle brown
He light on those shall bring him clown.
But see, who comes his news to show!
Malise! what tidings of the foe?'

VIII.

'At Doune, o'er many a spear and glaive
Two Barons proud their banners wave.
I saw the Moray's silver star,
And marked the sable pale of Mar.'
'By Alpine's soul, high tidings those!
I love to hear of worthy foes.
When move they on?' 'To-morrow's noon
Will see them here for battle boune.'
'Then shall it see a meeting stern!
But, for the place,--say, couldst thou learn
Nought of the friendly clans of Earn?
Strengthened by them, we well might bide
The battle on Benledi's side.
Thou couldst not?--well! Clan-Alpine's men
Shall man the Trosachs' shaggy glen;
Within Loch Katrine's gorge we'll fight,
All in our maids' and matrons' sight,
Each for his hearth and household fire,
Father for child, and son for sire Lover
for maid beloved!--But why
Is it the breeze affects mine eye?
Or dost thou come, ill-omened tear!

A messenger of doubt or fear?
No! sooner may the Saxon lance
Unfix Benledi from his stance,
Than doubt or terror can pierce through
The unyielding heart of Roderick Dhu!
'tis stubborn as his trusty targe.
Each to his post!--all know their charge.'
The pibroch sounds, the bands advance,
The broadswords gleam, the banners dance'
Obedient to the Chieftain's glance.--
I turn me from the martial roar
And seek Coir-Uriskin once more.

IX.

Where is the Douglas?--he is gone;
And Ellen sits on the gray stone
Fast by the cave, and makes her moan,
While vainly Allan's words of cheer
Are poured on her unheeding ear.
'He will return--dear lady, trust!--
With joy return;--he will--he must.
Well was it time to seek afar
Some refuge from impending war,
When e'en Clan-Alpine's rugged swarm
Are cowed by the approaching storm.
I saw their boats with many a light,
Floating the livelong yesternight,
Shifting like flashes darted forth
By the red streamers of the north;
I marked at morn how close they ride,
Thick moored by the lone islet's side,
Like wild ducks couching in the fen
When stoops the hawk upon the glen.
Since this rude race dare not abide
The peril on the mainland side,
Shall not thy noble father's care
Some safe retreat for thee prepare?'

X.

Ellen.

'No, Allan, no ' Pretext so kind
My wakeful terrors could not blind.
When in such tender tone, yet grave,
Douglas a parting blessing gave,
The tear that glistened in his eye
Drowned not his purpose fixed and high.
My soul, though feminine and weak,
Can image his; e'en as the lake,
Itself disturbed by slightest stroke.
Reflects the invulnerable rock.
He hears report of battle rife,
He deems himself the cause of strife.
I saw him redden when the theme
Turned, Allan, on thine idle dream
Of Malcolm Graeme in fetters bound,
Which I, thou saidst, about him wound.
Think'st thou he bowed thine omen aught?
O no' 't was apprehensive thought
For the kind youth,-- for Roderick too--
Let me be just--that friend so true;
In danger both, and in our cause!
Minstrel, the Douglas dare not pause.
Why else that solemn warning given,
'If not on earth, we meet in heaven!'
Why else, to Cambus-kenneth's fane,
If eve return him not again,
Am I to hie and make me known?
Alas! he goes to Scotland's throne,
Buys his friends' safety with his own;
He goes to do--what I had done,
Had Douglas' daughter been his son!'

XI.

'Nay, lovely Ellen!--dearest, nay!
If aught should his return delay,
He only named yon holy fane
As fitting place to meet again.
Be sure he's safe; and for the Graeme,--
Heaven's blessing on his gallant name!--

My visioned sight may yet prove true,
Nor bode of ill to him or you.
When did my gifted dream beguile?
Think of the stranger at the isle,
And think upon the harpings slow
That presaged this approaching woe!
Sooth was my prophecy of fear;
Believe it when it augurs cheer.
Would we had left this dismal spot!
Ill luck still haunts a fairy spot!
Of such a wondrous tale I know--
Dear lady, change that look of woe,
My harp was wont thy grief to cheer.'

Ellen.

'Well, be it as thou wilt;
I hear, But cannot stop the bursting tear.'
The Minstrel tried his simple art,
Rut distant far was Ellen's heart.

XII.

Ballad.

Alice Brand.

Merry it is in the good greenwood,
When the mavis and merle are singing,
When the deer sweeps by, and the hounds are in cry,
And the hunter's horn is ringing.

'O Alice Brand, my native land
Is lost for love of you;
And we must hold by wood and word,
As outlaws wont to do.

'O Alice, 't was all for thy locks so bright,
And 't was all for thine eyes so blue,
That on the night of our luckless flight
Thy brother bold I slew.

'Now must I teach to hew the beech
The hand that held the glaive,
For leaves to spread our lowly bed,
And stakes to fence our cave.

'And for vest of pall, thy fingers small,
That wont on harp to stray,
A cloak must shear from the slaughtered deer,
To keep the cold away.'

'O Richard! if my brother died,
'T was but a fatal chance;
For darkling was the battle tried,
And fortune sped the lance.

'If pall and vair no more I wear,
Nor thou the crimson sheen
As warm, we'll say, is the russet gray,
As gay the forest-green.

'And, Richard, if our lot be hard,
And lost thy native land,
Still Alice has her own Richard,
And he his Alice Brand.'

XIII.

Ballad Continued.

'tis merry, 'tis merry, in good greenwood;
So blithe Lady Alice is singing;
On the beech's pride, and oak's brown side,
Lord Richard's axe is ringing.

Up spoke the moody Elfin King,
Who woned within the hill,--
Like wind in the porch of a ruined church,
His voice was ghostly shrill.

'Why sounds yon stroke on beech and oak,
Our moonlight circle's screen?
Or who comes here to chase the deer,

Beloved of our Elfin Queen?
Or who may dare on wold to wear
The fairies' fatal green?

'Up, Urgan, up! to yon mortal hie,
For thou wert christened man;
For cross or sign thou wilt not fly,
For muttered word or ban.

'Lay on him the curse of the withered heart,
The curse of the sleepless eye;
Till he wish and pray that his life would part,
Nor yet find leave to die.'

XIV.

Ballad Continued.

'Tis merry, 'tis merry, in good greenwood,
Though the birds have stilled their singing;
The evening blaze cloth Alice raise,
And Richard is fagots bringing.

Up Urgan starts, that hideous dwarf,
Before Lord Richard stands,
And, as he crossed and blessed himself,
'I fear not sign,' quoth the grisly elf,
'That is made with bloody hands.'

But out then spoke she, Alice Brand,
That woman void of fear,--
'And if there 's blood upon his hand,
'Tis but the blood of deer.'

'Now loud thou liest, thou bold of mood!
It cleaves unto his hand,
The stain of thine own kindly blood,
The blood of Ethert Brand.'

Then forward stepped she, Alice Brand,
And made the holy sign,--
'And if there's blood on Richard's hand,

A spotless hand is mine.

'And I conjure thee, demon elf,
By Him whom demons fear,
To show us whence thou art thyself,
And what thine errand here?'

XV.

Ballad Continued.

"Tis merry, 'tis merry, in Fairy-land,
When fairy birds are singing,
When the court cloth ride by their monarch's side,
With bit and bridle ringing:

'And gayly shines the Fairy-land--
But all is glistening show,
Like the idle gleam that December's beam
Can dart on ice and snow.

'And fading, like that varied gleam,
Is our inconstant shape,
Who now like knight and lady seem,
And now like dwarf and ape.

'It was between the night and day,
When the Fairy King has power,
That I sunk down in a sinful fray,
And 'twixt life and death was snatched away
To the joyless Elfin bower.

'But wist I of a woman bold,
Who thrice my brow durst sign,
I might regain my mortal mould,
As fair a form as thine.'

She crossed him once--she crossed him twice--
That lady was so brave;
The fouler grew his goblin hue,
The darker grew the cave.

She crossed him thrice, that lady bold;
He rose beneath her hand
The fairest knight on Scottish mould,
Her brother, Ethert Brand!

Merry it is in good greenwood,
When the mavis and merle are singing,
But merrier were they in Dunfermline gray,
When all the bells were ringing.

XVI.

Just as the minstrel sounds were stayed,
A stranger climbed the steepy glade;
His martial step, his stately mien,
His hunting-suit of Lincoln green,
His eagle glance, remembrance claims--
'Tis Snowdoun's Knight, 'tis James Fitz-James.
Ellen beheld as in a dream,
Then, starting, scarce suppressed a scream:
'O stranger! in such hour of fear
What evil hap has brought thee here?'
'An evil hap how can it be
That bids me look again on thee?
By promise bound, my former guide
Met me betimes this morning-tide,
And marshalled over bank and bourne
The happy path of my return.'
'The happy path!--what! said he naught
Of war, of battle to be fought,
Of guarded pass?' 'No, by my faith!
Nor saw I aught could augur scathe.'
'O haste thee, Allan, to the kern:
Yonder his tartars I discern;
Learn thou his purpose, and conjure
That he will guide the stranger sure!--
What prompted thee, unhappy man?
The meanest serf in Roderick's clan
Had not been bribed, by love or fear,
Unknown to him to guide thee here.'

XVII.

'Sweet Ellen, dear my life must be,
Since it is worthy care from thee;
et life I hold but idle breath
When love or honor's weighed with death.
Then let me profit by my chance,
And speak my purpose bold at once.
I come to bear thee from a wild
Where ne'er before such blossom smiled,
By this soft hand to lead thee far
From frantic scenes of feud and war.
Near Bochastle my horses wait;
They bear us soon to Stirling gate.
I'll place thee in a lovely bower,
I'll guard thee like a tender flower--'
'O hush, Sir Knight! 't were female art,
To say I do not read thy heart;
Too much, before, my selfish ear
Was idly soothed my praise to hear.
That fatal bait hath lured thee back,
In deathful hour, o'er dangerous track;
And how, O how, can I atone
The wreck my vanity brought on!--
One way remains--I'll tell him all--
Yes! struggling bosom, forth it shall!
Thou, whose light folly bears the blame,
Buy thine own pardon with thy shame!
But first--my father is a man
Outlawed and exiled, under ban;
The price of blood is on his head,
With me 't were infamy to wed.
Still wouldst thou speak?--then hear the truth!
Fitz- James, there is a noble youth--
If yet he is!--exposed for me
And mine to dread extremity--
Thou hast the secret of my bears;
Forgive, be generous, and depart!'

XVIII.

Fitz-James knew every wily train

A lady's fickle heart to gain,
But here he knew and felt them vain.
There shot no glance from Ellen's eye,
To give her steadfast speech the lie;
In maiden confidence she stood,
Though mantled in her cheek the blood
And told her love with such a sigh
Of deep and hopeless agony,
As death had sealed her Malcolm's doom
And she sat sorrowing on his tomb.
Hope vanished from Fitz-James's eye,
But not with hope fled sympathy.
He proffered to attend her side,
As brother would a sister guide.
'O little know'st thou Roderick's heart!
Safer for both we go apart.
O haste thee, and from Allan learn
If thou mayst trust yon wily kern.'
With hand upon his forehead laid,
The conflict of his mind to shade,
A parting step or two he made;
Then, as some thought had crossed his brain
He paused, and turned, and came again.

XIX.

'Hear, lady, yet a parting word!--
It chanced in fight that my poor sword
Preserved the life of Scotland's lord.
This ring the grateful Monarch gave,
And bade, when I had boon to crave,
To bring it back, and boldly claim
The recompense that I would name.
Ellen, I am no courtly lord,
But one who lives by lance and sword,
Whose castle is his helm and shield,
His lordship the embattled field.
What from a prince can I demand,
Who neither reck of state nor land?
Ellen, thy hand--the ring is thine;
Each guard and usher knows the sign.
Seek thou the King without delay;

This signet shall secure thy way:
And claim thy suit, whate'er it be,
As ransom of his pledge to me.'
He placed the golden circlet on,
Paused--kissed her hand--and then was gone.
The aged Minstrel stood aghast,
So hastily Fitz-James shot past.
He joined his guide, and wending down
The ridges of the mountain brown,
Across the stream they took their way
That joins Loch Katrine to Achray.

XX

All in the Trosachs' glen was still,
Noontide was sleeping on the hill:
Sudden his guide whooped loud and high--
'Murdoch! was that a signal cry?'--
He stammered forth, 'I shout to scare
Yon raven from his dainty fare.'
He looked--he knew the raven's prey,
His own brave steed: 'Ah! gallant gray!
For thee--for me, perchance--'t were well
We ne'er had seen the Trosachs' dell.--
Murdoch, move first---but silently;
Whistle or whoop, and thou shalt die!'
Jealous and sullen on they fared,
Each silent, each upon his guard.

XXI.

Now wound the path its dizzy ledge
Around a precipice's edge,
When lo! a wasted female form,
Blighted by wrath of sun and storm,
In tattered weeds and wild array,
Stood on a cliff beside the way,
And glancing round her restless eye,
Upon the wood, the rock, the sky,
Seemed naught to mark, yet all to spy.
Her brow was wreathed with gaudy broom;

With gesture wild she waved a plume
Of feathers, which the eagles fling
To crag and cliff from dusky wing;
Such spoils her desperate step had sought,
Where scarce was footing for the goat.
The tartan plaid she first descried,
And shrieked till all the rocks replied;
As loud she laughed when near they drew,
For then the Lowland garb she knew;
And then her hands she wildly wrung,
And then she wept, and then she sung--
She sung!--the voice, in better time,
Perchance to harp or lute might chime;
And now, though strained and roughened, still
Rung wildly sweet to dale and hill.

XXII.

Song.

They bid me sleep, they bid me pray,
They say my brain is warped and wrung--
I cannot sleep on Highland brae,
I cannot pray in Highland tongue.
But were I now where Allan glides,
Or heard my native Devan's tides,
So sweetly would I rest, and pray
That Heaven would close my wintry day!

'Twas thus my hair they bade me braid,
They made me to the church repair;
It was my bridal morn they said,
And my true love would meet me there.
But woe betide the cruel guile
That drowned in blood the morning smile!
And woe betide the fairy dream!
I only waked to sob and scream.

XXIII.

'Who is this maid? what means her lay?

She hovers o'er the hollow way,
And flutters wide her mantle gray,
As the lone heron spreads his wing,
By twilight, o'er a haunted spring.'
''Tis Blanche of Devan,' Murdoch said,
'A crazed and captive Lowland maid,
Ta'en on the morn she was a bride,
When Roderick forayed Devan-side.
The gay bridegroom resistance made,
And felt our Chief's unconquered blade.
I marvel she is now at large,
But oft she 'scapes from Maudlin's charge.--
Hence, brain-sick fool!'--He raised his bow:--
'Now, if thou strik'st her but one blow,
I'll pitch thee from the cliff as far
As ever peasant pitched a bar!'
'Thanks, champion, thanks' the Maniac cried,
And pressed her to Fitz-James's side.
'See the gray pennons I prepare,
To seek my true love through the air!
I will not lend that savage groom,
To break his fall, one downy plume!
No!--deep amid disjointed stones,
The wolves shall batten on his bones,
And then shall his detested plaid,
By bush and brier in mid-air stayed,
Wave forth a banner fail and free,
Meet signal for their revelry.'

XXIV

'Hush thee, poor maiden, and be still!'
'O! thou look'st kindly, and I will.
Mine eye has dried and wasted been,
But still it loves the Lincoln green;
And, though mine ear is all unstrung,
Still, still it loves the Lowland tongue.

'For O my sweet William was forester true,
He stole poor Blanche's heart away!
His coat it was all of the greenwood hue,
And so blithely he trilled the Lowland lay!

'It was not that I meant to tell . . .
But thou art wise and guessest well.'
Then, in a low and broken tone,
And hurried note, the song went on.
Still on the Clansman fearfully
She fixed her apprehensive eye,
Then turned it on the Knight, and then
Her look glanced wildly o'er the glen.

XXV.

'The toils are pitched, and the stakes are set,--
Ever sing merrily, merrily;
The bows they bend, and the knives they whet,
Hunters live so cheerily.

It was a stag, a stag of ten,
Bearing its branches sturdily;
He came stately down the glen,--
Ever sing hardily, hardily.

'It was there he met with a wounded doe,
She was bleeding deathfully;
She warned him of the toils below,
O. so faithfully, faithfully!

'He had an eye, and he could heed,--
Ever sing warily, warily;
He had a foot, and he could speed,--
Hunters watch so narrowly.'

XXVI.

Fitz-James's mind was passion-tossed,
When Ellen's hints and fears were lost;
But Murdoch's shout suspicion wrought,
And Blanche's song conviction brought.
Not like a stag that spies the snare,
But lion of the hunt aware,
He waved at once his blade on high,

'Disclose thy treachery, or die!'
Forth at hell speed the Clansman flew,
But in his race his bow he drew.
The shaft just grazed Fitz-James's crest,
And thrilled in Blanche's faded breast.--
Murdoch of Alpine! prove thy speed,
For ne'er had Alpine's son such need;
With heart of fire, and foot of wind,
The fierce avenger is behind!
Fate judges of the rapid strife--
The forfeit death--the prize is life;
Thy kindred ambush lies before,
Close couched upon the heathery moor;
Them couldst thou reach!--it may not be
Thine ambushed kin thou ne'er shalt see,
The fiery Saxon gains on thee!--
Resistless speeds the deadly thrust,
As lightning strikes the pine to dust;
With foot and hand Fitz-James must strain
Ere he can win his blade again.
Bent o'er the fallen with falcon eye,
He grimly smiled to see him die,
Then slower wended back his way,
Where the poor maiden bleeding lay.

XXVII.

She sat beneath the birchen tree,
Her elbow resting on her knee;
She had withdrawn the fatal shaft,
And gazed on it, and feebly laughed;
Her wreath of broom and feathers gray,
Daggled with blood, beside her lay.
The Knight to stanch the life-stream tried,--
'Stranger, it is in vain!' she cried.
'This hour of death has given me more
Of reason's power than years before;
For, as these ebbing veins decay,
My frenzied visions fade away.
A helpless injured wretch I die,
And something tells me in thine eye
That thou wert mine avenger born.

Seest thou this tress?--O. still I 've worn
This little tress of yellow hair,
Through danger, frenzy, and despair!
It once was bright and clear as thine,
But blood and tears have dimmed its shine.
I will not tell thee when 't was shred,
Nor from what guiltless victim's head,--
My brain would turn!--but it shall wave
Like plumage on thy helmet brave,
Till sun and wind shall bleach the stain,
And thou wilt bring it me again.
I waver still. --O God! more bright
Let reason beam her parting light!--
O. by thy knighthood's honored sign,
And for thy life preserved by mine,
When thou shalt see a darksome man,
Who boasts him Chief of Alpine's Clan,
With tartars broad and shadowy plume,
And hand of blood, and brow of gloom
Be thy heart bold, thy weapon strong,
And wreak poor Blanche of Devan's wrong!--
They watch for thee by pass and fell . . .
Avoid the path . . . O God! . . . farewell.'

XXVIII.

A kindly heart had brave Fitz-James;
Fast poured his eyes at pity's claims;
And now, with mingled grief and ire,
He saw the murdered maid expire.
'God, in my need, be my relief,
As I wreak this on yonder Chief!'
A lock from Blanche's tresses fair
He blended with her bridegroom's hair;
The mingled braid in blood he dyed,
And placed it on his bonnet-side:
'By Him whose word is truth, I swear,
No other favour will I wear,
Till this sad token I imbrue
In the best blood of Roderick Dhu!--
But hark! what means yon faint halloo?
The chase is up,--but they shall know,

The stag at bay 's a dangerous foe.'
Barred from the known but guarded way,
Through copse and cliffs Fitz-James must stray,
And oft must change his desperate track,
By stream and precipice turned back.
Heartless, fatigued, and faint, at length,
From lack of food and loss of strength
He couched him in a thicket hoar
And thought his toils and perils o'er:--
'Of all my rash adventures past,
This frantic feat must prove the last!
Who e'er so mad but might have guessed
That all this Highland hornet's nest
Would muster up in swarms so soon
As e'er they heard of bands at Doune?--
Like bloodhounds now they search me out,--
Hark, to the whistle and the shout!--
If farther through the wilds I go,
I only fall upon the foe:
I'll couch me here till evening gray,
Then darkling try my dangerous way.'

XXIX.

The shades of eve come slowly down,
The woods are wrapt in deeper brown,
The owl awakens from her dell,
The fox is heard upon the fell;
Enough remains of glimmering light
To guide the wanderer's steps aright,
Yet not enough from far to show
His figure to the watchful foe.
With cautious step and ear awake,
He climbs the crag and threads the brake;
And not the summer solstice there
Tempered the midnight mountain air,
But every breeze that swept the wold
Benumbed his drenched limbs with cold.
In dread, in danger, and alone,
Famished and chilled, through ways unknown,
Tangled and steep, he journeyed on;
Till, as a rock's huge point he turned,

A watch-fire close before him burned.

XXX.

Beside its embers red and clear
Basked in his plaid a mountaineer;
And up he sprung with sword in hand,--
'Thy name and purpose! Saxon, stand!'
'A stranger.' 'What cost thou require?'
'Rest and a guide, and food and fire
My life's beset, my path is lost,
The gale has chilled my limbs with frost.'
'Art thou a friend to Roderick?' 'No.'
'Thou dar'st not call thyself a foe?'
'I dare! to him and all the band
He brings to aid his murderous hand.'
'Bold words!--but, though the beast of game
The privilege of chase may claim,
Though space and law the stag we lend
Ere hound we slip or bow we bend
Who ever recked, where, how, or when,
The prowling fox was trapped or slain?
Thus treacherous scouts,--yet sure they lie
Who say thou cam'st a secret spy!'--
'They do, by heaven!--come Roderick Dhu
And of his clan the boldest two
And let me but till morning rest,
I write the falsehood on their crest.'
If by the blaze I mark aright
Thou bear'st the belt and spur of Knight.'
'Then by these tokens mayst thou know
Each proud oppressor's mortal foe.'
'Enough, enough; sit down and share
A soldier's couch, a soldier's fare.'

XXXI..

He gave him of his Highland cheer,
The hardened flesh of mountain deer;
Dry fuel on the fire he laid,
And bade the Saxon share his plaid.

He tended him like welcome guest,
Then thus his further speech addressed:--
'Stranger, I am to Roderick Dhu
A clansman born, a kinsman true;
Each word against his honour spoke
Demands of me avenging stroke;
Yet more,--upon thy fate, 'tis said,
A mighty augury is laid.
It rests with me to wind my horn,--
Thou art with numbers overborne;
It rests with me, here, brand to brand,
Worn as thou art, to bid thee stand:
But, not for clan, nor kindred's cause,
Will I depart from honour's laws;
To assail a wearied man were shame,
And stranger is a holy name;
Guidance and rest, and food and fire,
In vain he never must require.
Then rest thee here till dawn of day;
Myself will guide thee on the way,
O'er stock and stone, through watch and ward,
Till past Clan- Alpine's outmost guard,
As far as Coilantogle's ford;
From thence thy warrant is thy sword.'
'I take thy courtesy, by heaven,
As freely as 'tis nobly given!'
Well, rest thee; for the bittern's cry
Sings us the lake's wild lullaby.'
With that he shook the gathered heath,
And spread his plaid upon the wreath;
And the brave foemen, side by side,
Lay peaceful down like brothers tried,
And slept until the dawning beam
Purpled the mountain and the stream.

CANTO FIFTH.

The Combat.

I.

Fair as the earliest beam of eastern light,
When first, by the bewildered pilgrim spied,
It smiles upon the dreary brow of night
And silvers o'er the torrent's foaming tide
And lights the fearful path on mountain-side,--
Fair as that beam, although the fairest far,
Giving to horror grace, to danger pride,
Shine martial Faith, and Courtesy's bright star
Through all the wreckful storms that cloud the brow of War.

II.

That early beam, so fair and sheen,
Was twinkling through the hazel screen
When, rousing at its glimmer red,
The warriors left their lowly bed,
Looked out upon the dappled sky,
Muttered their soldier matins try,
And then awaked their fire, to steal,
As short and rude, their soldier meal.
That o'er, the Gael around him threw
His graceful plaid of varied hue,
And, true to promise, led the way,
By thicket green and mountain gray.
A wildering path!--they winded now
Along the precipice's brow,
Commanding the rich scenes beneath,
The windings of the Forth and Teith,
And all the vales between that lie.
Till Stirling's turrets melt in sky;
Then, sunk in copse, their farthest glance
Gained not the length of horseman's lance.
'Twas oft so steep, the foot was as fain
Assistance from the hand to gain;

So tangled oft that, bursting through,
Each hawthorn shed her showers of dew,--
That diamond dew, so pure and clear,
It rivals all but Beauty's tear!

III.

At length they came where, stern and steep,
The hill sinks down upon the deep.
Here Vennachar in silver flows,
There, ridge on ridge, Benledi rose;
Ever the hollow path twined on,
Beneath steep hank and threatening stone;
A hundred men might hold the post
With hardihood against a host.
The rugged mountain's scanty cloak
Was dwarfish shrubs of birch and oak
With shingles bare, and cliffs between
And patches bright of bracken green,
And heather black, that waved so high,
It held the copse in rivalry.
But where the lake slept deep and still
Dank osiers fringed the swamp and hill;
And oft both path and hill were torn
Where wintry torrent down had borne
And heaped upon the cumbered land
Its wreck of gravel, rocks, and sand.
So toilsome was the road to trace
The guide, abating of his pace,
Led slowly through the pass's jaws
And asked Fitz-James by what strange cause
He sought these wilds, traversed by few
Without a pass from Roderick Dhu.

IV.

'Brave Gael, my pass, in danger tried
Hangs in my belt and by my side
Yet, sooth to tell,' the Saxon said,
'I dreamt not now to claim its aid.
When here, but three days since,

I came Bewildered in pursuit of game,
All seemed as peaceful and as still
As the mist slumbering on yon hill;
Thy dangerous Chief was then afar,
Nor soon expected back from war.
Thus said, at least, my mountain-guide,
Though deep perchance the villain lied.'
'Yet why a second venture try?'
'A warrior thou, and ask me why!--
Moves our free course by such fixed cause
As gives the poor mechanic laws?
Enough, I sought to drive away
The lazy hours of peaceful day;
Slight cause will then suffice to guide
A Knight's free footsteps far and wide,--
A falcon flown, a greyhound strayed,
The merry glance of mountain maid;
Or, if a path be dangerous known,
The danger's self is lure alone.'

V.

'Thy secret keep, I urge thee not;--
Yet, ere again ye sought this spot,
Say, heard ye naught of Lowland war,
Against Clan-Alpine, raised by Mar?'
'No, by my word;--of bands prepared
To guard King James's sports I heard;
Nor doubt I aught, but, when they hear
This muster of the mountaineer,
Their pennons will abroad be flung,
Which else in Doune had peaceful hung.'
'Free be they flung! for we were loath
Their silken folds should feast the moth.
Free be they flung!--as free shall wave
Clan-Alpine's pine in banner brave.
But, stranger, peaceful since you came,
Bewildered in the mountain-game,
Whence the bold boast by which you show
Vich-Alpine's vowed and mortal foe?'
'Warrior, but yester-morn I knew
Naught of thy Chieftain, Roderick Dhu,

Save as an outlawed desperate man,
The chief of a rebellious clan,
Who, in the Regent's court and sight,
With ruffian dagger stabbed a knight;
Yet this alone might from his part
Sever each true and loyal heart.'

VI.

Wrathful at such arraignment foul,
Dark lowered the clansman's sable scowl.
A space he paused, then sternly said,
'And heardst thou why he drew his blade?
Heardst thou that shameful word and blow
Brought Roderick's vengeance on his foe?
What recked the Chieftain if he stood
On Highland heath or Holy-Rood?
He rights such wrong where it is given,
If it were in the court of heaven.'
'Still was it outrage;--yet, 'tis true,
Not then claimed sovereignty his due;
While Albany with feeble hand
Held borrowed truncheon of command,
The young King, mewed in Stirling tower,
Was stranger to respect and power.
But then, thy Chieftain's robber life!--
Winning mean prey by causeless strife,
Wrenching from ruined Lowland swain
His herds and harvest reared in vain,--
Methinks a soul like thine should scorn
The spoils from such foul foray borne.'

VII.

The Gael beheld him grim the while,
And answered with disdainful smile:
'Saxon, from yonder mountain high,
I marked thee send delighted eye
Far to the south and east, where lay,
Extended in succession gay,
Deep waving fields and pastures green,

With gentle slopes and groves between:--
These fertile plains, that softened vale,
Were once the birthright of the Gael;
The stranger came with iron hand,
And from our fathers reft the land.
Where dwell we now? See, rudely swell
Crag over crag, and fell o'er fell.
Ask we this savage hill we tread
For fattened steer or household bread,
Ask we for flocks these shingles dry,
And well the mountain might reply,--
"To you, as to your sires of yore,
Belong the target and claymore!
I give you shelter in my breast,
Your own good blades must win the rest."
Pent in this fortress of the North,
Think'st thou we will not sally forth,
To spoil the spoiler as we may,
And from the robber rend the prey?
Ay, by my soul!--While on yon plain
The Saxon rears one shock of grain,
While of ten thousand herds there strays
But one along yon river's maze,--
The Gael, of plain and river heir,
Shall with strong hand redeem his share.
Where live the mountain Chiefs who hold
That plundering Lowland field and fold
Is aught but retribution true?
Seek other cause 'gainst Roderick Dhu.'

VIII.

Answered Fitz-James: 'And, if I sought,
Think'st thou no other could be brought?
What deem ye of my path waylaid?
My life given o'er to ambuscade?'
'As of a meed to rashness due:
Hadst thou sent warning fair and true,--
I seek my hound or falcon strayed,
I seek, good faith, a Highland maid,--
Free hadst thou been to come and go;
But secret path marks secret foe.

Nor yet for this, even as a spy,
Hadst thou, unheard, been doomed to die,
Save to fulfil an augury.'
'Well, let it pass; nor will I now
Fresh cause of enmity avow
To chafe thy mood and cloud thy brow.
Enough, I am by promise tied
To match me with this man of pride:
Twice have I sought Clan-Alpine's glen
In peace; but when I come again,
I come with banner, brand, and bow,
As leader seeks his mortal foe.
For love-lore swain in lady's bower
Ne'er panted for the appointed hour
As I, until before me stand
This rebel Chieftain and his band!'

IX.

'Have then thy wish!'--He whistled shrill
And he was answered from the hill;
Wild as the scream of the curlew,
From crag to crag the signal flew.
Instant, through copse and heath, arose
Bonnets and spears and bended bows
On right, on left, above, below,
Sprung up at once the lurking foe;
From shingles gray their lances start,
The bracken bush sends forth the dart,
The rushes and the willow-wand
Are bristling into axe and brand,
And every tuft of broom gives life
'To plaided warrior armed for strife.
That whistle garrisoned the glen
At once with full five hundred men,
As if the yawning hill to heaven
A subterranean host had given.
Watching their leader's beck and will,
All silent there they stood and still.
Like the loose crags whose threatening mass
Lay tottering o'er the hollow pass,
As if an infant's touch could urge

Their headlong passage down the verge,
With step and weapon forward flung,
Upon the mountain-side they hung.
The Mountaineer cast glance of pride
Along Benledi's living side,
Then fixed his eye and sable brow
Full on Fitz-James: 'How say'st thou now?
These are Clan-Alpine's warriors true;
And, Saxon,--I am Roderick Dhu!'

X.

Fitz-James was brave:--though to his heart
The life-blood thrilled with sudden start,
He manned himself with dauntless air,
Returned the Chief his haughty stare,
His back against a rock he bore,
And firmly placed his foot before:--
'Come one, come all! this rock shall fly
From its firm base as soon as I.'
Sir Roderick marked,--and in his eyes
Respect was mingled with surprise,
And the stern joy which warriors feel
In foeman worthy of their steel.
Short space he stood--then waved his hand:
Down sunk the disappearing band;
Each warrior vanished where he stood,
In broom or bracken, heath or wood;
Sunk brand and spear and bended bow,
In osiers pale and copses low;
It seemed as if their mother Earth
Had swallowed up her warlike birth.
The wind's last breath had tossed in air
Pennon and plaid and plumage fair,--
The next but swept a lone hill-side
Where heath and fern were waving wide:
The sun's last glance was glinted back
From spear and glaive, from targe and jack,--
The next, all unreflected, shone
On bracken green and cold gray stone.

XI.

Fitz-James looked round,--yet scarce believed
The witness that his sight received;
Such apparition well might seem
Delusion of a dreadful dream.
Sir Roderick in suspense he eyed,
And to his look the Chief replied:
'Fear naught--nay, that I need not say
But--doubt not aught from mine array.
Thou art my guest;--I pledged my word
As far as Coilantogle ford:
Nor would I call a clansman's brand
For aid against one valiant hand,
Though on our strife lay every vale
Rent by the Saxon from the Gael.
So move we on;--I only meant
To show the reed on which you leant,
Deeming this path you might pursue
Without a pass from Roderick Dhu.'
They moved;--I said Fitz-James was brave
As ever knight that belted glaive,
Yet dare not say that now his blood
Kept on its wont and tempered flood,
As, following Roderick's stride, he drew
That seeming lonesome pathway through,
Which yet by fearful proof was rife
With lances, that, to take his life,
Waited but signal from a guide,
So late dishonored and defied.
Ever, by stealth, his eye sought round
The vanished guardians of the ground,
And stir'd from copse and heather deep
Fancy saw spear and broadsword peep,
And in the plover's shrilly strain
The signal whistle heard again.
Nor breathed he free till far behind
The pass was left; for then they wind
Along a wide and level green,
Where neither tree nor tuft was seen,
Nor rush nor bush of broom was near,
To hide a bonnet or a spear.

XII.

The Chief in silence strode before,
And reached that torrent's sounding shore,
Which, daughter of three mighty lakes,
From Vennachar in silver breaks,
Sweeps through the plain, and ceaseless mines
On Bochastle the mouldering lines,
Where Rome, the Empress of the world,
Of yore her eagle wings unfurled.
And here his course the Chieftain stayed,
Threw down his target and his plaid,
And to the Lowland warrior said:
'Bold Saxon! to his promise just,
Vich-Alpine has discharged his trust.
This murderous Chief, this ruthless man,
This head of a rebellious clan,
Hath led thee safe, through watch and ward,
Far past Clan-Alpine's outmost guard.
Now, man to man, and steel to steel,
A Chieftain's vengeance thou shalt feel.
See, here all vantageless I stand,
Armed like thyself with single brand;
For this is Coilantogle ford,
And thou must keep thee with thy sword.'

XIII.

The Saxon paused: 'I ne'er delayed,
When foeman bade me draw my blade;
Nay more, brave Chief, I vowed thy death;
Yet sure thy fair and generous faith,
And my deep debt for life preserved,
A better meed have well deserved:
Can naught but blood our feud atone?
Are there no means?'--' No, stranger, none!
And hear,--to fire thy flagging zeal,--
The Saxon cause rests on thy steel;
For thus spoke Fate by prophet bred
Between the living and the dead:"
Who spills the foremost foeman's life,

His party conquers in the strife."'
'Then, by my word,' the Saxon said,
"The riddle is already read.
Seek yonder brake beneath the cliff,--
There lies Red Murdoch, stark and stiff.
Thus Fate hath solved her prophecy;
Then yield to Fate, and not to me.
To James at Stirling let us go,
When, if thou wilt be still his foe,
Or if the King shall not agree
To grant thee grace and favor free,
I plight mine honor, oath, and word
That, to thy native strengths restored,
With each advantage shalt thou stand
That aids thee now to guard thy land.'

XIV.

Dark lightning flashed from Roderick's eye:
'Soars thy presumption, then, so high,
Because a wretched kern ye slew,
Homage to name to Roderick Dhu?
He yields not, he, to man nor Fate!
Thou add'st but fuel to my hate;--
My clansman's blood demands revenge.
Not yet prepared?--By heaven, I change
My thought, and hold thy valor light
As that of some vain carpet knight,
Who ill deserved my courteous care,
And whose best boast is but to wear
A braid of his fair lady's hair.' 'I thank thee,
Roderick, for the word!
It nerves my heart, it steels my sword;
For I have sworn this braid to stain
In the best blood that warms thy vein.
Now, truce, farewell! and, rush, begone!--
Yet think not that by thee alone,
Proud Chief! can courtesy be shown;
Though not from copse, or heath, or cairn,
Start at my whistle clansmen stern,
Of this small horn one feeble blast
Would fearful odds against thee cast.

But fear not -- doubt not--which thou wilt--
We try this quarrel hilt to hilt.'
Then each at once his falchion drew,
Each on the ground his scabbard threw
Each looked to sun and stream and plain
As what they ne'er might see again;
Then foot and point and eye opposed,
In dubious strife they darkly closed.

XV.

Ill fared it then with Roderick Dhu,
That on the field his targe he threw,
Whose brazen studs and tough bull-hide
Had death so often dashed aside;
For, trained abroad his arms to wield
Fitz-James's blade was sword and shield.
He practised every pass and ward,
To thrust, to strike, to feint, to guard;
While less expert, though stronger far,
The Gael maintained unequal war.
Three times in closing strife they stood
And thrice the Saxon blade drank blood;
No stinted draught, no scanty tide,
The gushing flood the tartars dyed.
Fierce Roderick felt the fatal drain,
And showered his blows like wintry rain;
And, as firm rock or castle-roof
Against the winter shower is proof,
The foe, invulnerable still,
Foiled his wild rage by steady skill;
Till, at advantage ta'en, his brand
Forced Roderick's weapon from his hand,
And backward borne upon the lea,
Brought the proud Chieftain to his knee.

XVI.

Now yield thee, or by Him who made
The world, thy heart's blood dyes my blade!;
'Thy threats, thy mercy, I defy!

Let recreant yield, who fears to die.'
Like adder darting from his coil,
Like wolf that dashes through the toil,
Like mountain-cat who guards her young,
Full at Fitz-James's throat he sprung;
Received, but recked not of a wound,
And locked his arms his foeman round.
Now, gallant Saxon, hold thine own!
No maiden's hand is round thee thrown!
That desperate grasp thy frame might feel
Through bars of brass and triple steel!
They tug, they strain! down, down they go,
The Gael above, Fitz-James below.
The Chieftain's gripe his throat compressed,
His knee was planted on his breast;
His clotted locks he backward threw,
Across his brow his hand he drew,
From blood and mist to clear his sight,
Then gleamed aloft his dagger bright!
But hate and fury ill supplied
The stream of life's exhausted tide,
And all too late the advantage came,
To turn the odds of deadly game;
For, while the dagger gleamed on high,
Reeled soul and sense, reeled brain and eye.
Down came the blow! but in the heath
The erring blade found bloodless sheath.
The struggling foe may now unclasp
The fainting Chief's relaxing grasp;
Unwounded from the dreadful close,
But breathless all, Fitz-James arose.

XVII.

He faltered thanks to Heaven for life,
Redeemed, unhoped, from desperate strife;
Next on his foe his look he cast,
Whose every gasp appeared his last
In Roderick's gore he dipped the braid,--
'Poor Blanche! thy wrongs are dearly paid;
Yet with thy foe must die, or live,
The praise that faith and valor give.'

With that he blew a bugle note,
Undid the collar from his throat,
Unbonneted, and by the wave
Sat down his brow and hands to rave.
Then faint afar are heard the feet
Of rushing steeds in gallop fleet;
The sounds increase, and now are seen
Four mounted squires in Lincoln green;
Two who bear lance, and two who lead
By loosened rein a saddled steed;
Each onward held his headlong course,
And by Fitz-James reined up his horse,--
With wonder viewed the bloody spot,--
'Exclaim not, gallants ' question not.--
You, Herbert and Luffness, alight
And bind the wounds of yonder knight;
Let the gray palfrey bear his weight,
We destined for a fairer freight,
And bring him on to Stirling straight;
I will before at better speed,
To seek fresh horse and fitting weed.
The sun rides high;--I must be boune
To see the archer-game at noon;
But lightly Bayard clears the lea.--
De Vaux and Herries. follow me.

XVIII.

'Stand, Bayard, stand!'--the steed obeyed,
With arching neck and bended head,
And glancing eye and quivering ear,
As if he loved his lord to hear.
No foot Fitz-James in stirrup stayed,
No grasp upon the saddle laid,
But wreathed his left hand in the mane,
And lightly bounded from the plain,
Turned on the horse his armed heel,
And stirred his courage with the steel.
Bounded the fiery steed in air,
The rider sat erect and fair,
Then like a bolt from steel crossbow
Forth launched, along the plain they go.

They dashed that rapid torrent through,
And up Carhonie's hill they flew;
Still at the gallop pricked the Knight,
His merrymen followed as they might.
Along thy banks, swift Teith! they ride,
And in the race they mock thy tide;
Torry and Lendrick now are past,
And Deanstown lies behind them cast;
They rise, the bannered towers of Doune,
They sink in distant woodland soon;
Blair-Drummond sees the hoofs strike fire,
They sweep like breeze through Ochtertyre;
They mark just glance and disappear
The lofty brow of ancient Kier;
They bathe their coursers' sweltering sides
Dark Forth! amid thy sluggish tides,
And on the opposing shore take ground
With plash, with scramble, and with bound.
Right-hand they leave thy cliffs, Craig-Forth!
And soon the bulwark of the North,
Gray Stirling, with her towers and town,
Upon their fleet career looked clown.

XIX.

As up the flinty path they strained,
Sudden his steed the leader reined;
A signal to his squire he flung,
Who instant to his stirrup sprung:--
'Seest thou, De Vaux, yon woodsman gray,
Who townward holds the rocky way,
Of stature tall and poor array?
Mark'st thou the firm, yet active stride,
With which he scales the mountain-side?
Know'st thou from whence he comes, or whom?'
'No, by my word;--a burly groom
He seems, who in the field or chase
A baron's train would nobly grace--'
'Out, out, De Vaux! can fear supply,
And jealousy, no sharper eye?
Afar, ere to the hill he drew,
That stately form and step I knew;

Like form in Scotland is not seen,
Treads not such step on Scottish green.
'Tis James of Douglas, by Saint Serle!
The uncle of the banished Earl.
Away, away, to court, to show
The near approach of dreaded foe:
The King must stand upon his guard;
Douglas and he must meet prepared.'
Then right-hand wheeled their steeds, and straight
They won the Castle's postern gate.

XX.

The Douglas, who had bent his way
From Cambus-kenneth's abbey gray,
Now, as he climbed the rocky shelf,
Held sad communion with himself:--
'Yes! all is true my fears could frame;
A prisoner lies the noble Graeme,
And fiery Roderick soon will feel
The vengeance of the royal steel.
I, only I, can ward their fate,--
God grant the ransom come not late!
The Abbess hath her promise given,
My child shall be the bride of Heaven;--
Be pardoned one repining tear!
For He who gave her knows how dear,
How excellent!--but that is by,
And now my business is--to die.--
Ye towers! within whose circuit dread
A Douglas by his sovereign bled;
And thou, O sad and fatal mound!
That oft hast heard the death-axe sound.
As on the noblest of the land
Fell the stern headsmen's bloody hand,--
The dungeon, block, and nameless tomb
Prepare--for Douglas seeks his doom!
But hark! what blithe and jolly peal
Makes the Franciscan steeple reel?
And see! upon the crowded street,
In motley groups what masquers meet!
Banner and pageant, pipe and drum,

And merry morrice-dancers come.
I guess, by all this quaint array,
The burghers hold their sports to-day.
James will be there; he loves such show,
Where the good yeoman bends his bow,
And the tough wrestler foils his foe,
As well as where, in proud career,
The high-born filter shivers spear.
I'll follow to the Castle-park,
And play my prize;--King James shall mark
If age has tamed these sinews stark,
Whose force so oft in happier days
His boyish wonder loved to praise.'

XXI.

The Castle gates were open flung,
The quivering drawbridge rocked and rung,
And echoed loud the flinty street
Beneath the coursers' clattering feet,
As slowly down the steep descent
Fair Scotland's King and nobles went,
While all along the crowded way
Was jubilee and loud huzza.
And ever James was bending low
To his white jennet's saddle-bow,
Doffing his cap to city dame,
Who smiled and blushed for pride and shame.
And well the simperer might be vain,--
He chose the fairest of the train.
Gravely he greets each city sire,
Commends each pageant's quaint attire,
Gives to the dancers thanks aloud,
And smiles and nods upon the crowd,
Who rend the heavens with their acclaims,--
'Long live the Commons' King, King James!'
Behind the King thronged peer and knight,
And noble dame and damsel bright,
Whose fiery steeds ill brooked the stay
Of the steep street and crowded way.
But in the train you might discern
Dark lowering brow and visage stern;

There nobles mourned their pride restrained,
And the mean burgher's joys disdained;
And chiefs, who, hostage for the* clan,
Were each from home a banished man,
There thought upon their own gray tower,
Their waving woods, their feudal power,
And deemed themselves a shameful part
Of pageant which they cursed in heart.

XXII.

Now, in the Castle-park, drew out
Their checkered bands the joyous rout.
There morricers, with bell at heel
And blade in hand, their mazes wheel;
But chief, beside the butts, there stand
Bold Robin Hood and all his band,--
Friar Tuck with quarterstaff and cowl,
Old Scathelocke with his surly scowl,
Maid Marian, fair as ivory bone,
Scarlet, and Mutch, and Little John;
Their bugles challenge all that will,
In archery to prove their skill.
The Douglas bent a bow of might,--
His first shaft centred in the white,
And when in turn he shot again,
His second split the first in twain.
From the King's hand must Douglas take
A silver dart, the archers' stake;
Fondly he watched, with watery eye,
Some answering glance of sympathy,--
No kind emotion made reply!
Indifferent as to archer wight,
The monarch gave the arrow bright.

XXIII.

Now, clear the ring! for, hand to hand,
The manly wrestlers take their stand.
Two o'er the rest superior rose,
And proud demanded mightier foes,--

Nor called in vain, for Douglas came.--
For life is Hugh of Larbert lame;
Scarce better John of Alloa's fare,
Whom senseless home his comrades bare.
Prize of the wrestling match, the King
To Douglas gave a golden ring,
While coldly glanced his eye of blue,
As frozen drop of wintry dew.
Douglas would speak, but in his breast
His struggling soul his words suppressed;
Indignant then he turned him where
Their arms the brawny yeomen bare,
To hurl the massive bar in air.
When each his utmost strength had shown,
The Douglas rent an earth-fast stone
From its deep bed, then heaved it high,
And sent the fragment through the sky
A rood beyond the farthest mark;
And still in Stirling's royal park,
The gray-haired sires, who know the past,
To strangers point the Douglas cast,
And moralize on the decay
Of Scottish strength in modern day.

XXIV.

The vale with loud applauses rang,
The Ladies' Rock sent back the clang.
The King, with look unmoved, bestowed
A purse well filled with pieces broad.
Indignant smiled the Douglas proud,
And threw the gold among the crowd,
Who now with anxious wonder scan,
And sharper glance, the dark gray man;
Till whispers rose among the throng,
That heart so free, and hand so strong,
Must to the Douglas blood belong.
The old men marked and shook the head,
To see his hair with silver spread,
And winked aside, and told each son
Of feats upon the English done,
Ere Douglas of the stalwart hand

Was exiled from his native land.
The women praised his stately form,
Though wrecked by many a winter's storm;
The youth with awe and wonder saw
His strength surpassing Nature's law.
Thus judged, as is their wont, the crowd
Till murmurs rose to clamours loud.
But not a glance from that proud ring
Of peers who circled round the King
With Douglas held communion kind,
Or called the banished man to mind;
No, not from those who at the chase
Once held his side the honoured place,
Begirt his board, and in the field
Found safety underneath his shield;
For he whom royal eyes disown,
When was his form to courtiers known!

XXV.

The Monarch saw the gambols flag
And bade let loose a gallant stag,
Whose pride, the holiday to crown,
Two favorite greyhounds should pull down,
That venison free and Bourdeaux wine
Might serve the archery to dine.
But Lufra,--whom from Douglas' side
Nor bribe nor threat could e'er divide,
The fleetest hound in all the North,--
Brave Lufra saw, and darted forth.
She left the royal hounds midway,
And dashing on the antlered prey,
Sunk her sharp muzzle in his flank,
And deep the flowing life-blood drank.
The King's stout huntsman saw the sport
By strange intruder broken short,
Came up, and with his leash unbound
In anger struck the noble hound.
The Douglas had endured, that morn,
The King's cold look, the nobles' scorn,
And last, and worst to spirit proud,
Had borne the pity of the crowd;

But Lufra had been fondly bred,
To share his board, to watch his bed,
And oft would Ellen Lufra's neck
In maiden glee with garlands deck;
They were such playmates that with name
Of Lufra Ellen's image came.
His stifled wrath is brimming high,
In darkened brow and flashing eye;
As waves before the bark divide,
The crowd gave way before his stride;
Needs but a buffet and no more,
The groom lies senseless in his gore.
Such blow no other hand could deal,
Though gauntleted in glove of steel.

XXVI.

Then clamored loud the royal train,
And brandished swords and staves amain,
But stern the Baron's warning:
'Back! Back, on your lives, ye menial pack!
Beware the Douglas.--Yes! behold,
King James! The Douglas, doomed of old,
And vainly sought for near and far,
A victim to atone the war,
A willing victim, now attends,
Nor craves thy grace but for his friends.--'
'Thus is my clemency repaid?
Presumptuous Lord!' the Monarch said:
'Of thy misproud ambitious clan,
Thou, James of Bothwell, wert the man,
The only man, in whom a foe
My woman-mercy would not know;
But shall a Monarch's presence brook
Injurious blow and haughty look?--
What ho! the Captain of our Guard!
Give the offender fitting ward.--
Break off the sports!'--for tumult rose,
And yeomen 'gan to bend their bows,
'Break off the sports!' he said and frowned,
'And bid our horsemen clear the ground.'

XXVII.

Then uproar wild and misarray
Marred the fair form of festal day.
The horsemen pricked among the crowd,
Repelled by threats and insult loud;
To earth are borne the old and weak,
The timorous fly, the women shriek;
With flint, with shaft, with staff, with bar,
The hardier urge tumultuous war.
At once round Douglas darkly sweep
The royal spears in circle deep,
And slowly scale the pathway steep,
While on the rear in thunder pour
The rabble with disordered roar
With grief the noble Douglas saw
The Commons rise against the law,
And to the leading soldier said:
'Sir John of Hyndford, 'twas my blade
That knighthood on thy shoulder laid;
For that good deed permit me then
A word with these misguided men.--

XXVIII,

'Hear, gentle friends, ere yet for me
Ye break the bands of fealty.
My life, my honour, and my cause,
I tender free to Scotland's laws.
Are these so weak as must require
'Fine aid of your misguided ire?
Or if I suffer causeless wrong,
Is then my selfish rage so strong,
My sense of public weal so low,
That, for mean vengeance on a foe,
Those cords of love I should unbind
Which knit my country and my kind?
O no! Believe, in yonder tower
It will not soothe my captive hour,
To know those spears our foes should dread
For me in kindred gore are red:

'To know, in fruitless brawl begun,
For me that mother wails her son,
For me that widow's mate expires,
For me that orphans weep their sires,
That patriots mourn insulted laws,
And curse the Douglas for the cause.
O let your patience ward such ill,
And keep your right to love me still I'

XXIX.

The crowd's wild fury sunk again
In tears, as tempests melt in rain.
With lifted hands and eyes, they prayed
For blessings on his generous head
Who for his country felt alone,
And prized her blood beyond his own.
Old men upon the verge of life
Blessed him who stayed the civil strife;
And mothers held their babes on high,
The self-devoted Chief to spy,
Triumphant over wrongs and ire,
To whom the prattlers owed a sire.
Even the rough soldier's heart was moved;
As if behind some bier beloved,
With trailing arms and drooping head,
The Douglas up the hill he led,
And at the Castle's battled verge,
With sighs resigned his honoured charge.

XXX.

The offended Monarch rode apart,
With bitter thought and swelling heart,
And would not now vouchsafe again
Through Stirling streets to lead his train.
'O Lennox, who would wish to rule
This changeling crowd, this common fool?
Hear'st thou,' he said, 'the loud acclaim
With which they shout the Douglas name?
With like acclaim the vulgar throat

Strained for King James their morning note;
With like acclaim they hailed the day
When first I broke the Douglas sway;
And like acclaim would Douglas greet
If he could hurl me from my seat.
Who o'er the herd would wish to reign,
Fantastic, fickle, fierce, and vain?
Vain as the leaf upon the stream,
And fickle as a changeful dream;
Fantastic as a woman's mood,
And fierce as Frenzy's fevered blood.
Thou many-headed monster-thing,
O who would wish to be thy king?--

XXXI..

'But soft! what messenger of speed
Spurs hitherward his panting steed?
I guess his cognizance afar--
What from our cousin, John of Mar?'
'He prays, my liege, your sports keep bound
Within the safe and guarded ground;
For some foul purpose yet unknown,--
Most sure for evil to the throne,--
The outlawed Chieftain, Roderick Dhu,
Has summoned his rebellious crew;
'Tis said, in James of Bothwell's aid
These loose banditti stand arrayed.
The Earl of Mar this morn from Doune
To break their muster marched, and soon
Your Grace will hear of battle fought;
But earnestly the Earl besought,
Till for such danger he provide,
With scanty train you will not ride.'

XXXII.

'Thou warn'st me I have done amiss,--
I should have earlier looked to this;
I lost it in this bustling day.--
Retrace with speed thy former way;

Spare not for spoiling of thy steed,
The best of mine shall be thy meed.
Say to our faithful Lord of Mar,
We do forbid the intended war;
Roderick this morn in single fight
Was made our prisoner by a knight,
And Douglas hath himself and cause
Submitted to our kingdom's laws.
The tidings of their leaders lost
Will soon dissolve the mountain host,
Nor would we that the vulgar feel,
For their Chief's crimes, avenging steel.
Bear Mar our message, Braco, fly!'
He turned his steed,--'My liege, I hie,
Yet ere I cross this lily lawn
I fear the broadswords will be drawn.'
The turf the flying courser spurned,
And to his towers the King returned.

XXXIII.

Ill with King James's mood that day
Suited gay feast and minstrel lay;
Soon were dismissed the courtly throng,
And soon cut short the festal song.
Nor less upon the saddened town
The evening sunk in sorrow down.
The burghers spoke of civil jar,
Of rumoured feuds and mountain war,
Of Moray, Mar, and Roderick Dhu,
All up in arms;--the Douglas too,
They mourned him pent within the hold,
'Where stout Earl William was of old.'--
And there his word the speaker stayed,
And finger on his lip he laid,
Or pointed to his dagger blade.
But jaded horsemen from the west
At evening to the Castle pressed,
And busy talkers said they bore
Tidings of fight on Katrine's shore;
At noon the deadly fray begun,
And lasted till the set of sun.

Thus giddy rumor shook the town,
Till closed the Night her pennons brown.

The Lady of the Lake

CANTO SIXTH.

The Guard-room.

I.

The sun, awakening, through the smoky air
Of the dark city casts a sullen glance,
Rousing each caitiff to his task of care,
Of sinful man the sad inheritance;
Summoning revellers from the lagging dance,
Scaring the prowling robber to his den;
Gilding on battled tower the warder's lance,
And warning student pale to leave his pen,
And yield his drowsy eyes to the kind nurse of men.

What various scenes, and O, what scenes of woe,
Are witnessed by that red and struggling beam!
The fevered patient, from his pallet low,
Through crowded hospital beholds it stream;
The ruined maiden trembles at its gleam,
The debtor wakes to thought of gyve and jail,
'The love-lore wretch starts from tormenting dream:
The wakeful mother, by the glimmering pale,
Trims her sick infant's couch, and soothes his feeble wail.

II.

At dawn the towers of Stirling rang
With soldier-step and weapon-clang,
While drums with rolling note foretell
Relief to weary sentinel.
Through narrow loop and casement barred,
The sunbeams sought the Court of Guard,
And, struggling with the smoky air,
Deadened the torches' yellow glare.
In comfortless alliance shone
The lights through arch of blackened stone,
And showed wild shapes in garb of war,
Faces deformed with beard and scar,

All haggard from the midnight watch,
And fevered with the stern debauch;
For the oak table's massive board,
Flooded with wine, with fragments stored,
And beakers drained, and cups o'erthrown,
Showed in what sport the night had flown.
Some, weary, snored on floor and bench;
Some labored still their thirst to quench;
Some, chilled with watching, spread their hands
O'er the huge chimney's dying brands,
While round them, or beside them flung,
At every step their harness rung.

III.

These drew not for their fields the sword,
Like tenants of a feudal lord,
Nor owned the patriarchal claim
Of Chieftain in their leader's name;
Adventurers they, from far who roved,
To live by battle which they loved.
There the Italian's clouded face,
The swarthy Spaniard's there you trace;
The mountain-loving Switzer there
More freely breathed in mountain-air;
The Fleming there despised the soil
That paid so ill the labourer's toil;
Their rolls showed French and German name;
And merry England's exiles came,
To share, with ill-concealed disdain,
Of Scotland's pay the scanty gain.
All brave in arms, well trained to wield
The heavy halberd, brand, and shield;
In camps licentious, wild, and bold;
In pillage fierce and uncontrolled;
And now, by holytide and feast,
From rules of discipline released.

IV.

'They held debate of bloody fray,

Fought 'twixt Loch Katrine and Achray.
Fierce was their speech, and mid their words
'Their hands oft grappled to their swords;
Nor sunk their tone to spare the ear
Of wounded comrades groaning near,
Whose mangled limbs and bodies gored
Bore token of the mountain sword,
Though, neighbouring to the Court of Guard,
Their prayers and feverish wails were heard,--
Sad burden to the ruffian joke,
And savage oath by fury spoke!--
At length up started John of Brent,
A yeoman from the banks of Trent;
A stranger to respect or fear,
In peace a chaser of the deer,
In host a hardy mutineer,
But still the boldest of the crew
When deed of danger was to do.
He grieved that day their games cut short,
And marred the dicer's brawling sport,
And shouted loud, 'Renew the bowl!
And, while a merry catch I troll,
Let each the buxom chorus bear,
Like brethren of the brand and spear.'

V.

Soldier's Song.

Our vicar still preaches that Peter and Poule
Laid a swinging long curse on the bonny brown bowl,
That there 's wrath and despair in the jolly black-jack,
And the seven deadly sins in a flagon of sack;
Yet whoop, Barnaby! off with thy liquor,
Drink upsees out, and a fig for the vicar!

Our vicar he calls it damnation to sip
The ripe ruddy dew of a woman's dear lip,
Says that Beelzebub lurks in her kerchief so sly,
And Apollyon shoots darts from her merry black eye;
Yet whoop, Jack! kiss Gillian the quicker,
Till she bloom like a rose, and a fig for the vicar!

Our vicar thus preaches,--and why should he not?
For the dues of his cure are the placket and pot;
And 'tis right of his office poor laymen to lurch
Who infringe the domains of our good Mother Church.
Yet whoop, bully-boys! off with your liquor,
Sweet Marjorie 's the word and a fig for the vicar!

VI.

The warder's challenge, heard without,
Stayed in mid-roar the merry shout.
A soldier to the portal went,--
'Here is old Bertram, sirs, of Ghent;
And--beat for jubilee the drum!--
A maid and minstrel with him come.'
Bertram, a Fleming, gray and scarred,
Was entering now the Court of Guard,
A harper with him, and, in plaid
All muffled close, a mountain maid,
Who backward shrunk to 'scape the view
Of the loose scene and boisterous crew.
'What news?' they roared:--' I only know,
From noon till eve we fought with foe,
As wild and as untamable
As the rude mountains where they dwell;
On both sides store of blood is lost,
Nor much success can either boast.'--
'But whence thy captives, friend? such spoil
As theirs must needs reward thy toil.
Old cost thou wax, and wars grow sharp;
Thou now hast glee-maiden and harp!
Get thee an ape, and trudge the land,
The leader of a juggler band.'

VII.

'No, comrade;--no such fortune mine.
After the fight these sought our line,
That aged harper and the girl,
And, having audience of the Earl,

Mar bade I should purvey them steed,
And bring them hitherward with speed.
Forbear your mirth and rude alarm,
For none shall do them shame or harm.--
'Hear ye his boast?' cried John of Brent,
Ever to strife and jangling bent;
'Shall he strike doe beside our lodge,
And yet the jealous niggard grudge
To pay the forester his fee?
I'll have my share howe'er it be,
Despite of Moray, Mar, or thee.'
Bertram his forward step withstood;
And, burning in his vengeful mood,
Old Allan, though unfit for strife,
Laid hand upon his dagger-knife;
But Ellen boldly stepped between,
And dropped at once the tartan screen:--
So, from his morning cloud, appears
The sun of May through summer tears.
The savage soldiery, amazed,
As on descended angel gazed;
Even hardy Brent, abashed and tamed,
Stood half admiring, half ashamed.

VIII.

Boldly she spoke: 'Soldiers, attend!
My father was the soldier's friend,
Cheered him in camps, in marches led,
And with him in the battle bled.
Not from the valiant or the strong
Should exile's daughter suffer wrong.'
Answered De Brent, most forward still
In every feat or good or ill:
'I shame me of the part I played;
And thou an outlaw's child, poor maid!
An outlaw I by forest laws,
And merry Needwood knows the cause.
Poor Rose,--if Rose be living now,'--
He wiped his iron eye and brow,--
'Must bear such age, I think, as thou.--
Hear ye, my mates! I go to call

The Captain of our watch to hall:
There lies my halberd on the floor;
And he that steps my halberd o'er,
To do the maid injurious part,
My shaft shall quiver in his heart!
Beware loose speech, or jesting rough;
Ye all know John de Brent. Enough.'

IX.

Their Captain came, a gallant young,--
Of Tullibardine's house he sprung,--
Nor wore he yet the spurs of knight;
Gay was his mien, his humor light
And, though by courtesy controlled,
Forward his speech, his bearing bold.
The high-born maiden ill could brook
The scanning of his curious look
And dauntless eye:--and yet, in sooth
Young Lewis was a generous youth;
But Ellen's lovely face and mien
Ill suited to the garb and scene,
Might lightly bear construction strange,
And give loose fancy scope to range.
'Welcome to Stirling towers, fair maid!
Come ye to seek a champion's aid,
On palfrey white, with harper hoar,
Like errant damosel of yore?
Does thy high quest a knight require,
Or may the venture suit a squire?'
Her dark eye flashed;--she paused and sighed:--
'O what have I to do with pride!--
Through scenes of sorrow, shame, and strife,
A suppliant for a father's life,
I crave an audience of the King.
Behold, to back my suit, a ring,
The royal pledge of grateful claims,
Given by the Monarch to Fitz-James.'

X.

The signet-ring young Lewis took
With deep respect and altered look,
And said: 'This ring our duties own;
And pardon, if to worth unknown,
In semblance mean obscurely veiled,
Lady, in aught my folly failed.
Soon as the day flings wide his gates,
The King shall know what suitor waits.
Please you meanwhile in fitting bower
Repose you till his waking hour.
Female attendance shall obey
Your hest, for service or array.
Permit I marshal you the way.'
But, ere she followed, with the grace
And open bounty of her race,
She bade her slender purse be shared
Among the soldiers of the guard.
The rest with thanks their guerdon took,
But Brent, with shy and awkward look,
On the reluctant maiden's hold
Forced bluntly back the proffered gold:--
'Forgive a haughty English heart,
And O, forget its ruder part!

The vacant purse shall be my share,
Which in my barrel-cap I'll bear,
Perchance, in jeopardy of war,
Where gayer crests may keep afar.'
With thanks--'twas all she could--the maid
His rugged courtesy repaid.

XI.

When Ellen forth with Lewis went,
Allan made suit to John of Brent:--
'My lady safe, O let your grace
Give me to see my master's face!
His minstrel I,--to share his doom
Bound from the cradle to the tomb.
Tenth in descent, since first my sires
Waked for his noble house their Iyres,
Nor one of all the race was known

But prized its weal above their own.
With the Chief's birth begins our care;
Our harp must soothe the infant heir,
Teach the youth tales of fight, and grace
His earliest feat of field or chase;
In peace, in war, our rank we keep,
We cheer his board, we soothe his sleep,
Nor leave him till we pour our verse--
A doleful tribute!--o'er his hearse.
Then let me share his captive lot;
It is my right,--deny it not!'
'Little we reck,' said John of Brent,
'We Southern men, of long descent;
Nor wot we how a name--a word--
Makes clansmen vassals to a lord:
Yet kind my noble landlord's part,--
God bless the house of Beaudesert!
And, but I loved to drive the deer
More than to guide the labouring steer,
I had not dwelt an outcast here.
Come, good old Minstrel, follow me;
Thy Lord and Chieftain shalt thou see.'

XII.

Then, from a rusted iron hook,
A bunch of ponderous keys he took,
Lighted a torch, and Allan led
Through grated arch and passage dread.
Portals they passed, where, deep within,
Spoke prisoner's moan and fetters' din;
Through rugged vaults, where, loosely stored,
Lay wheel, and axe, and headsmen's sword,
And many a hideous engine grim,
For wrenching joint and crushing limb,
By artists formed who deemed it shame
And sin to give their work a name.
They halted at a Iow-browed porch,
And Brent to Allan gave the torch,
While bolt and chain he backward rolled,
And made the bar unhasp its hold.
They entered:--'twas a prison-room

Of stern security and gloom,
Yet not a dungeon; for the day
Through lofty gratings found its way,
And rude and antique garniture
Decked the sad walls and oaken floor,
Such as the rugged days of old
Deemed fit for captive noble's hold.
'Here,' said De Brent, 'thou mayst remain
Till the Leech visit him again.
Strict is his charge, the,warders tell,
To tend the noble prisoner well.'
Retiring then the bolt he drew,
And the lock's murmurs growled anew.
Rousing at the sound, from lowly bed
A captive feebly raised his head.
The wondering Minstrel looked, and knew--
Not his dear lord, but Roderick Dhu!
For, come from where Clan-Alpine fought,
They, erring, deemed the Chief he sought.

XIII.

As the tall ship, whose lofty prore
Shall never stem the billows more,
Deserted by her gallant band,
Amid the breakers lies astrand,--
So on his couch lay Roderick Dhu!
And oft his fevered limbs he threw
In toss abrupt, as when her sides
Lie rocking in the advancing tides,
That shake her frame with ceaseless beat,
Yet cannot heave her from her seat;--
O, how unlike her course at sea!
Or his free step on hill and lea!--
Soon as the Minstrel he could scan,--
'What of thy lady?--of my clan?--
My mother?--Douglas?--tell me all!
Have they been ruined in my fall?
Ah, yes! or wherefore art thou here?
Yet speak,--speak boldly,--do not fear.'--
For Allan, who his mood well knew,
Was choked with grief and terror too.--

'Who fought?--who fled?--Old man, be brief;--
Some might,--for they had lost their Chief.
Who basely live?--who bravely died?'
'O, calm thee, Chief!' the Minstrel cried,
'Ellen is safe!' 'For that thank Heaven!'
'And hopes are for the Douglas given;--
The Lady Margaret, too, is well;
And, for thy clan,--on field or fell,
Has never harp of minstrel told
Of combat fought so true and bold.
Thy stately Pine is yet unbent,
Though many a goodly bough is rent.'

XIV.

The Chieftain reared his form on high,
And fever's fire was in his eye;
But ghastly, pale, and livid streaks
Checkered his swarthy brow and cheeks.
'Hark, Minstrel! I have heard thee play,
With measure bold on festal day,
In yon lone isle,--again where ne'er
Shall harper play or warrior hear!--
That stirring air that peals on high,
O'er Dermid's race our victory.--
Strike it!--and then,--for well thou canst,--
Free from thy minstrel-spirit glanced,
Fling me the picture of the fight,
When met my clan the Saxon might.
I'll listen, till my fancy hears
The clang of swords' the crash of spears!
These grates, these walls, shall vanish then
For the fair field of fighting men,
And my free spirit burst away,
As if it soared from battle fray.'
The trembling Bard with awe obeyed,--
Slow on the harp his hand he laid;
But soon remembrance of the sight
He witnessed from the mountain's height,
With what old Bertram told at night,
Awakened the full power of song,
And bore him in career along;--

As shallop launched on river's tide,
'That slow and fearful leaves the side,
But, when it feels the middle stream,
Drives downward swift as lightning's beam.

XV.

Battle of Beal' An Duine.

'The Minstrel came once more to view
The eastern ridge of Benvenue,
For ere he parted he would say
Farewell to lovely loch Achray
Where shall he find, in foreign land,
So lone a lake, so sweet a strand!--
There is no breeze upon the fern,
No ripple on the lake,
Upon her eyry nods the erne,
The deer has sought the brake;
The small birds will not sing aloud,
The springing trout lies still,
So darkly glooms yon thunder-cloud,
That swathes, as with a purple shroud,
Benledi's distant hill.
Is it the thunder's solemn sound
That mutters deep and dread,
Or echoes from the groaning ground
The warrior's measured tread?
Is it the lightning's quivering glance
That on the thicket streams,
Or do they flash on spear and lance
The sun's retiring beams?--
I see the dagger-crest of Mar,
I see the Moray's silver star,
Wave o'er the cloud of Saxon war,
That up the lake comes winding far!

To hero boune for battle-strife,
Or bard of martial lay,
'Twere worth ten years of peaceful life,
One glance at their array!

XVI.

'Their light-armed archers far and near
Surveyed the tangled ground,
Their centre ranks, with pike and spear,
A twilight forest frowned,
Their barded horsemen in the rear
The stern battalia crowned.
No cymbal clashed, no clarion rang,
Still were the pipe and drum;
Save heavy tread, and armor's clang,
The sullen march was dumb.
There breathed no wind their crests to shake,
Or wave their flags abroad;
Scarce the frail aspen seemed to quake
That shadowed o'er their road.
Their vaward scouts no tidings bring,
Can rouse no lurking foe,
Nor spy a trace of living thing,
Save when they stirred the roe;
The host moves like a deep-sea wave,
Where rise no rocks its pride to brave
High-swelling, dark, and slow.
The lake is passed, and now they gain
A narrow and a broken plain,
Before the Trosachs' rugged jaws;
And here the horse and spearmen pause
While, to explore the dangerous glen
Dive through the pass the archer-men.

XVII.

'At once there rose so wild a yell
Within that dark and narrow dell,
As all the fiends from heaven that fell
Had pealed the banner-cry of hell!
Forth from the pass in tumult driven,
Like chaff before the wind of heaven,
The archery appear:
For life! for life! their flight they ply--
And shriek, and shout, and battle-cry,

And plaids and bonnets waving high,
And broadswords flashing to the sky,
Are maddening in the rear.
Onward they drive in dreadful race,
Pursuers and pursued;
Before that tide of flight and chase,
How shall it keep its rooted place,
The spearmen's twilight wood?-- "
"Down, down," cried Mar, "your lances down'
Bear back both friend and foe! "--
Like reeds before the tempest's frown,
That serried grove of lances brown
At once lay levelled low;
And closely shouldering side to side,
The bristling ranks the onset bide.-- "
"We'll quell the savage mountaineer,
As their Tinchel cows the game!
They come as fleet as forest deer,
We'll drive them back as tame."

XVIII.

'Bearing before them in their course
The relics of the archer force,
Like wave with crest of sparkling foam,
Right onward did Clan-Alpine come.
Above the tide, each broadsword bright
Was brandishing like beam of light,
Each targe was dark below;
And with the ocean's mighty swing,
When heaving to the tempest's wing,
They hurled them on the foe.
I heard the lance's shivering crash,
As when the whirlwind rends the ash;
I heard the broadsword's deadly clang,
As if a hundred anvils rang!
But Moray wheeled his rearward rank
Of horsemen on Clan-Alpine's flank,--
"My banner-man, advance!
I see," he cried, "their column shake.
Now, gallants! for your ladies' sake,
Upon them with the lance!"--

The horsemen dashed among the rout,
As deer break through the broom;

Their steeds are stout, their swords are out,
They soon make lightsome room.
Clan-Alpine's best are backward borne--
Where, where was Roderick then!
One blast upon his bugle-horn
Were worth a thousand men.
And refluent through the pass of fear
The battle's tide was poured;
Vanished the Saxon's struggling spear,
Vanished the mountain-sword.
As Bracklinn's chasm, so black and steep,
Receives her roaring linn
As the dark caverns of the deep
Suck the wild whirlpool in,
So did the deep and darksome pass
Devour the battle's mingled mass;
None linger now upon the plain
Save those who ne'er shall fight again.

XIX.

'Now westward rolls the battle's din,
That deep and doubling pass within.--
Minstrel, away! the work of fate
Is bearing on; its issue wait,
Where the rude Trosachs' dread defile
Opens on Katrine's lake and isle.
Gray Benvenue I soon repassed,
Loch Katrine lay beneath me cast.
The sun is set;--the clouds are met,
The lowering scowl of heaven
An inky hue of livid blue
To the deep lake has given;
Strange gusts of wind from mountain glen
Swept o'er the lake, then sunk again.
I heeded not the eddying surge,
Mine eye but saw the Trosachs' gorge,
Mine ear but heard that sullen sound,
Which like an earthquake shook the ground,

And spoke the stern and desperate strife
That parts not but with parting life,
Seeming, to minstrel ear, to toll
The dirge of many a passing soul.
Nearer it comes--the dim-wood glen
The martial flood disgorged again,
But not in mingled tide;
The plaided warriors of the North
High on the mountain thunder forth
And overhang its side,
While by the lake below appears
The darkening cloud of Saxon spears.
At weary bay each shattered band,
Eying their foemen, sternly stand;
Their banners stream like tattered sail,
That flings its fragments to the gale,
And broken arms and disarray
Marked the fell havoc of the day.

XX.

'Viewing the mountain's ridge askance,
The Saxons stood in sullen trance,
Till Moray pointed with his lance,
And cried: "Behold yon isle!--
See! none are left to guard its strand
But women weak, that wring the hand:
'Tis there of yore the robber band
Their booty wont to pile;--
My purse, with bonnet-pieces store,
To him will swim a bow-shot o'er,
And loose a shallop from the shore.
Lightly we'll tame the war-wolf then,
Lords of his mate, and brood, and den."
Forth from the ranks a spearman sprung,
On earth his casque and corselet rung,
He plunged him in the wave:--
All saw the deed,--the purpose knew,
And to their clamors Benvenue
A mingled echo gave;
The Saxons shout, their mate to cheer,
The helpless females scream for fear

And yells for rage the mountaineer.
'T was then, as by the outcry riven,
Poured down at once the lowering heaven:
A whirlwind swept Loch Katrine's breast,
Her billows reared their snowy crest.
Well for the swimmer swelled they high,
To mar the Highland marksman's eye;
For round him showered, mid rain and hail,
The vengeful arrows of the Gael.
In vain.--He nears the isle--and lo!
His hand is on a shallop's bow.
Just then a flash of lightning came,
It tinged the waves and strand with flame;
I marked Duncraggan's widowed dame,
Behind an oak I saw her stand,
A naked dirk gleamed in her hand:--
It darkened,--but amid the moan
Of waves I heard a dying groan;--
Another flash!--the spearman floats
A weltering corse beside the boats,
And the stern matron o'er him stood,
Her hand and dagger streaming blood.

XXI.

"'Revenge! revenge!" the Saxons cried,
The Gaels' exulting shout replied.
Despite the elemental rage,
Again they hurried to engage;
But, ere they closed in desperate fight,
Bloody with spurring came a knight,
Sprung from his horse, and from a crag
Waved 'twixt the hosts a milk-white flag.
Clarion and trumpet by his side
Rung forth a truce-note high and wide,
While, in the Monarch's name, afar
A herald's voice forbade the war,
For Bothwell's lord and Roderick bold
Were both, he said, in captive hold.'--
But here the lay made sudden stand,
The harp escaped the Minstrel's hand!
Oft had he stolen a glance, to spy

How Roderick brooked his minstrelsy:
At first, the Chieftain, to the chime,
With lifted hand kept feeble time;
That motion ceased,--yet feeling strong
Varied his look as changed the song;
At length, no more his deafened ear
The minstrel melody can hear;
His face grows sharp,--his hands are clenched'
As if some pang his heart-strings wrenched;
Set are his teeth, his fading eye
Is sternly fixed on vacancy;
Thus, motionless and moanless, drew
His parting breath stout Roderick Dhu!--
Old Allan-bane looked on aghast,
While grim and still his spirit passed;
But when he saw that life was fled,
He poured his wailing o'er the dead.

XXII.

Lament.

'And art thou cold and lowly laid,
Thy foeman's dread, thy people's aid,
Breadalbane's boast, Clan-Alpine's shade!
For thee shall none a requiem say?--
For thee, who loved the minstrel's lay,
For thee, of Bothwell's house the stay,
The shelter of her exiled line,
E'en in this prison-house of thine,
I'll wail for Alpine's honored Pine!

'What groans shall yonder valleys fill!
What shrieks of grief shall rend yon hill!
What tears of burning rage shall thrill,
When mourns thy tribe thy battles done,
Thy fall before the race was won,
Thy sword ungirt ere set of sun!
There breathes not clansman of thy line,
But would have given his life for thine.
O, woe for Alpine's honoured Pine!

'Sad was thy lot on mortal stage!--
The captive thrush may brook the cage,
The prisoned eagle dies for rage.
Brave spirit, do Dot scorn my strain!
And, when its notes awake again,
Even she, so long beloved in vain,
Shall with my harp her voice combine,
And mix her woe and tears with mine,
To wail Clan-Alpine's honoured Pine.'

XXIII.

Ellen the while, with bursting heart,
Remained in lordly bower apart,
Where played, with many-coloured gleams,
Through storied pane the rising beams.
In vain on gilded roof they fall,
And lightened up a tapestried wall,
And for her use a menial train
A rich collation spread in vain.
The banquet proud, the chamber gay,
Scarce drew one curious glance astray;
Or if she looked, 't was but to say,
With better omen dawned the day
In that lone isle, where waved on high
The dun-deer's hide for canopy;
Where oft her noble father shared
The simple meal her care prepared,
While Lufra, crouching by her side,
Her station claimed with jealous pride,
And Douglas, bent on woodland game,
Spoke of the chase to Malcolm Graeme,
Whose answer, oft at random made,
The wandering of his thoughts betrayed.
Those who such simple joys have known
Are taught to prize them when they 're gone.
But sudden, see, she lifts her head;
The window seeks with cautious tread.
What distant music has the power
To win her in this woful hour?
'T was from a turret that o'erhung
Her latticed bower, the strain was sung.

XXIV.

Lay of the Imprisoned Huntsman.

'My hawk is tired of perch and hood,
My idle greyhound loathes his food,
My horse is weary of his stall,
And I am sick of captive thrall.
I wish I were as I have been,
Hunting the hart in forest green,
With bended bow and bloodhound free,
For that's the life is meet for me.

I hate to learn the ebb of time
From yon dull steeple's drowsy chime,
Or mark it as the sunbeams crawl,
Inch after inch, along the wall.
The lark was wont my matins ring,
The sable rook my vespers sing;
These towers, although a king's they be,
Have not a hall of joy for me.

No more at dawning morn I rise,
And sun myself in Ellen's eyes,
Drive the fleet deer the forest through,
And homeward wend with evening dew;
A blithesome welcome blithely meet,
And lay my trophies at her feet,
While fled the eve on wing of glee,--
That life is lost to love and me!'

XXV.

The heart-sick lay was hardly said,
The listener had not turned her head,
It trickled still, the starting tear,
When light a footstep struck her ear,
And Snowdoun's graceful Knight was near.
She turned the hastier, lest again
The prisoner should renew his strain.

'O welcome, brave Fitz-James!' she said;
'How may an almost orphan maid
Pay the deep debt--' 'O say not so!
To me no gratitude you owe.
Not mine, alas! the boon to give,
And bid thy noble father live;
I can but be thy guide, sweet maid,
With Scotland's King thy suit to aid.
No tyrant he, though ire and pride
May lay his better mood aside.
Come, Ellen, come! 'tis more than time,
He holds his court at morning prime.'
With heating heart, and bosom wrung,
As to a brother's arm she clung.
Gently he dried the falling tear,
And gently whispered hope and cheer;
Her faltering steps half led, half stayed,
Through gallery fair and high arcade,
Till at his touch its wings of pride
A portal arch unfolded wide.

XXVI.

Within 't was brilliant all and light,
A thronging scene of figures bright;
It glowed on Ellen's dazzled sight,
As when the setting sun has given
Ten thousand hues to summer even,
And from their tissue fancy frames
Aerial knights and fairy dames.
Still by Fitz-James her footing staid;
A few faint steps she forward made,
Then slow her drooping head she raised,
And fearful round the presence gazed;
For him she sought who owned this state,
The dreaded Prince whose will was fate!--
She gazed on many a princely port
Might well have ruled a royal court;
On many a splendid garb she gazed,--
Then turned bewildered and amazed,
For all stood bare; and in the room
Fitz-James alone wore cap and plume.

To him each lady's look was lent,
On him each courtier's eye was bent;
Midst furs and silks and jewels sheen,
He stood, in simple Lincoln green,
The centre of the glittering ring,--
And Snowdoun's Knight is Scotland's King!

XXVII.

As wreath of snow on mountain-breast
Slides from the rock that gave it rest,
Poor Ellen glided from her stay,
And at the Monarch's feet she lay;
No word her choking voice commands,--
She showed the ring,--she clasped her hands.
O, not a moment could he brook,
The generous Prince, that suppliant look!
Gently he raised her,--and, the while,
Checked with a glance the circle's smile;
Graceful, but grave, her brow he kissed,
And bade her terrors be dismissed:--
'Yes, fair; the wandering poor
Fitz-James The fealty of Scotland claims.
To him thy woes, thy wishes, bring;
He will redeem his signet ring.
Ask naught for Douglas;--yester even,
His Prince and he have much forgiven;
Wrong hath he had from slanderous tongue,
I, from his rebel kinsmen, wrong.
We would not, to the vulgar crowd,
Yield what they craved with clamor loud;
Calmly we heard and judged his cause,
Our council aided and our laws.
I stanched thy father's death-feud stern
With stout De Vaux and gray Glencairn;
And Bothwell's Lord henceforth we own
The friend and bulwark of our throne.--
But, lovely infidel, how now?
What clouds thy misbelieving brow?
Lord James of Douglas, lend thine aid;
Thou must confirm this doubting maid.'

XXVIII.

Then forth the noble Douglas sprung,
And on his neck his daughter hung.
The Monarch drank, that happy hour,
The sweetest, holiest draught of Power,--
When it can say with godlike voice,
Arise, sad Virtue, and rejoice!
Yet would not James the general eye
On nature's raptures long should pry;
He stepped between--' Nay, Douglas, nay,
Steal not my proselyte away!
The riddle 'tis my right to read,
That brought this happy chance to speed.
Yes, Ellen, when disguised I stray
In life's more low but happier way,
'Tis under name which veils my power
Nor falsely veils,--for Stirling's tower
Of yore the name of Snowdoun claims,
And Normans call me James Fitz-James.
Thus watch I o'er insulted laws,
Thus learn to right the injured cause.'
Then, in a tone apart and low,--
'Ah, little traitress! none must know
What idle dream, what lighter thought
What vanity full dearly bought,
Joined to thine eye's dark witchcraft, drew
My spell-bound steps to Benvenue
In dangerous hour, and all but gave
Thy Monarch's life to mountain glaive!'
Aloud he spoke: 'Thou still cost hold
That little talisman of gold,
Pledge of my faith, Fitz-James's ring,--
What seeks fair Ellen of the King?'

XXIX.

Full well the conscious maiden guessed
He probed the weakness of her breast;
But with that consciousness there came
A lightening of her fears for Graeme,

And more she deemed the Monarch's ire
Kindled 'gainst him who for her sire
Rebellious broadsword boldly drew;
And, to her generous feeling true,
She craved the grace of Roderick Dhu.
'Forbear thy suit;--the King of kings
Alone can stay life's parting wings.
I know his heart, I know his hand,
Have shared his cheer, and proved his brand;
My fairest earldom would I give
To bid Clan- Alpine's Chieftain live!--
Hast thou no other boon to crave?
No other captive friend to save?'
Blushing, she turned her from the King,
And to the Douglas gave the ring,
As if she wished her sire to speak
The suit that stained her glowing cheek.
'Nay, then, my pledge has lost its force,
And stubborn justice holds her course.
Malcolm, come forth!'--and, at the word,
Down kneeled the Graeme to Scotland's Lord.
'For thee, rash youth, no suppliant sues,
From thee may Vengeance claim her dues,
Who, nurtured underneath our smile,
Hast paid our care by treacherous wile,
And sought amid thy faithful clan
A refuge for an outlawed man,
Dishonoring thus thy loyal name.--
Fetters and warder for the Graeme!'
His chain of gold the King unstrung,
The links o'er Malcolm's neck he flung,
Then gently drew the glittering band,
And laid the clasp on Ellen's hand.

Harp of the North, farewell! The hills grow dark,
On purple peaks a deeper shade descending;
In twilight copse the glow-worm lights her spark,
The deer, half seen, are to the covert wending.
Resume thy wizard elm! the fountain lending,
And the wild breeze, thy wilder minstrelsy;
Thy numbers sweet with nature's vespers blending,
With distant echo from the fold and lea,
And herd-boy's evening pipe, and hum of housing bee.

Yet, once again, farewell, thou Minstrel Harp!
Yet, once again, forgive my feeble sway,
And little reck I of the censure sharp
May idly cavil at an idle lay.
Much have I owed thy strains on life's long way,
Through secret woes the world has never known,
When on the weary night dawned wearier day,
And bitterer was the grief devoured alone.--
That I o'erlive such woes, Enchantress! is thine own.

Hark! as my lingering footsteps slow retire,
Some Spirit of the Air has waked thy string!
'Tis now a seraph bold, with touch of fire,
'Tis now the brush of Fairy's frolic wing.
Receding now, the dying numbers ring
Fainter and fainter down the rugged dell;
And now the mountain breezes scarcely bring
A wandering witch-note of the distant spell--
And now, 'tis silent all!--Enchantress, fare thee well!

Lightning Source UK Ltd.
Milton Keynes UK
22 February 2010

150451UK00001B/223/A